The Wild Adventures

of Robin and Summer

The Wild Adventures of Robin and Summer

Denny Lynch

Published by
TEAM DML Inc

CONTENTS

Dedicated to mom, dad, Ashley, Ryan, Kelly, and of course, Robin and Summer.

Prologue
Three Years Ago

The room she was staying in was unfamiliar. The wallpaper was old and bland. Her bed had no plushness, and it was covered by metal grates. The aroma in the room had the scents of past patients. It smelled of illness and despair. Not exactly welcoming.

An array of veterinarians and medical staff shuffled in and out of the room. They knew something was wrong with her. She felt something was wrong. She felt old, tired, and unwell. Her eyes grew weary from cataracts. Her hearing was no longer sharp. But that was nothing new. She's felt that way for a few years now; it came with age. But in the past week, she felt all her symptoms had multiplied.

"Come on, Zoey, time for a walk."

The young employee at the boarding facility tried to coax her into leaving the crate, but Zoey lacked the motivation. After so many years of life, she felt the end approaching. It was better this way; some dogs fear being alone for that last moment, but not Zoey. She didn't want to die around her beloved family.

The employee gave up and went to go find the lead veterinarian. At that moment, Zoey closed her eyes. Memories came to the forefront. The good memories. The ones that make life most fulfilling.

She thought about the endless amount of times, as a puppy, she would relieve herself on the floors and carpets of

1

her new home. Her owners were young at the time too. They were just married when they adopted Zoey. She was only a few months old; she couldn't remember her life before the adoption. Zoey only had beautiful memories of two newly-weds bonded by love. They had spent the summer months fixing up the new house. They did everything from freshly painting the walls to tiling the kitchen and bathrooms. They also installed new flooring in every room. Upstairs it was new wall-to-wall carpeting, downstairs, they nailed in knotty pine planking. There were also deliveries and lots of them. New furniture sets, televisions, wall art, and window drapes. Every penny, nickel, and dime they had was used to beautify the home.

And she was a menace to it all at first. When they were gone, she would chew up their new pillow sets. She would claw at the strands and fuzzies of their new rugs, creating rigid holes. There were days she would abandon her chew toys to gnaw and teeth on the wooden ends of their custom-built king bed. One time she tried hopping up on a windowsill to see the birds flying in their backyard. Unfortunately, the bold act resulted in her accidentally knocking over a lamp given to them by their new neighbor as a housewarming gift.

And when she finally got into the backyard through the unfinished doggy door to chase the birds, she also managed to scoot through an opening in the fence. She was lost for several hours, but her beloved married couple, Mitchell and Francine, spent those hours searching for her around the neighborhood. They finally found Zoey wandering in a neighborhood park, drinking from a pond. Instead of fierce reprimanding, they hugged her with love. They were glad they found her safe and unharmed.

She became better with training over time. Less pee and poop in the house. Less scratching up the rugs and door frames. She went from sleeping in the doggy pen to sleeping at the end of her owner's bed. Mitchell's calves became her pillow, while Francine's feet would be tickled by her fluffy tail. The bed arrangement wasn't ideal, but the couple grew accustomed to Zoey's presence. They loved her too much to shoo her away.

One of her favorite memories was long sunset walks with Mitchell and Francine. They would talk about things she did not understand, but it didn't matter. The sweet sounds of their conversations as they went from sidewalk to sidewalk, park to park, and lawn to lawn, made her feel a sense of jubilance. A sense of *home*.

Soon, a few years into her life as a member of their small family, the walks became less frequent. Things were changing. Francine had a large bump growing from her stomach as if she were ballooning. Soon, she couldn't take Zoey on walks, leaving the responsibility to Mitchell. When she sniffed the scents of Francine, she could also sense the presence of someone else. *Two* something elses.

Her owners kept using the word *babies*. And then everything in the house was being changed again. The guest bedroom was repainted with splashes of blue on one side and pink on the other. Cribs were assembled, high chairs were positioned, and tiny clothing sets were purchased. Something

3

exciting was happening. A new beginning of sorts. A welcoming.

And just like that, Zoey was introduced to two new humans. Two baby twins, a boy and a girl. She feared the presence of these humans would steal the affections of Mitchell and Francine. But instead, it only multiplied the love of their family. In fact, the babies became a forever important part of Zoey's life.

Zoey bonded strongly with these beautiful children. When the babies were old enough to walk, which was more like stumbling, they would laugh and giggle endlessly as they played with her. The playtime started a little rough and uncoordinated; the girl baby would try to grab Zoey's tail, and the boy baby would sometimes drool on her face when he tried to hug her. However, Zoey tolerated it all, and soon the playtime became less of a nuisance and more fun. Playtime sessions included games of fetch, chase, and tug of war. And that was just a handful of Zoey's favorites.

Another favorite memory was the day Mitchell and Francine brought her on a boat to go fishing with the kids. It was a sunny morning on the lake. The small waves rolled smoothly, and the air was enlightening and fresh. Mitchell helmed the small cruiser while Francine held onto the kids in the back. Zoey made her way to the boat's bow and held her head high into the wind. Her tongue wagged against the breeze, and the sun warmed her coat as wisps of water touched her body. She smiled through it all. The day ended with Zoey swimming with the toddlers and the parents for the first time. It was one of the best days of her life.

Smaller moments were memorable too. When the toddlers, now talkative and adventurous, had a birthday party, they snuck Zoey some frosted vanilla cake. It was a fraction of a slice, but it was the best thing she had ever tasted. And then she ate some leftover steak at a Fourth of July barbecue years later. Again, the meaty taste of the sirloin was heavenly.

A few months after that barbecue, Zoey was hurt jumping into a pile of autumn leaves; her paw had snagged on a thorny vine. She recovered by the side of the children, who refused to leave her alone for days. They even missed school to be with Zoey as her paw healed.

She watched the twins carve pumpkins for Halloween decorations. And when Halloween arrived, the paw was ready to be walked on again. Mitchell, Francine, and the kids took her trick-or-treating. The boy was dressed in a homemade Batman costume, while the girl was dressed as an astronaut with bedazzled flowers on her helmet. They dressed Zoey in a 'dog mummy' costume, using leftover bandage tape from her paw accident.

A cherished and unforgettable memory was one Christmas Eve night not too long ago. The children were taller and bigger now, spoke clearly like adults, and would walk Zoey around the neighborhood alone. On that night, all four of them took Zoey out for a Christmas Eve stroll. It was cold but delightful. Everything appeared magical. All the homes were lit up with decorations, and carolers stood singing at doorsteps. Despite losing some of her vision and hearing that year, she still experienced the Christmas spirit in that walk.

That evening ended with all of them gathering around the living room fireplace. The fire's warmth contrasted perfectly with the cold outdoors. And to their delight, it started to snow. Zoey watched the snowflakes fall for hours while cozied on Francine's lap. The following day, she had the joy of observing the children's excitement as they opened their presents. And then, of course, they opened presents for Zoey. Each year she was given new chew toys or a new doggy sweater. That year was no different, except for the addition of another gift. Both children unwrapped it: a framed portrait of all five of them. They probably thought Zoey did not understand this gift, but she did. She most certainly did. It was the best gift of all because it was a gift of love.

So many memories, including road trips, birthday parties, and countless hours of playing fetch. And then there was the first time her paws felt the sand of a beach, not to be outdone by the feeling of walking in crunchy snow after a winter blizzard. All of these moments were special, and they were all experienced by these four human beings. She loved them so much.

Now they were away on a trip. It was a crowded, fast-paced place with roller coasters and rides. No place for a dog, but Zoey understood. And it was better this way. She didn't want to die in their presence. It would be too much. And she knew whoever they adopted next would be loved unconditionally as she was.

Zoey blinked and closed her eyes one last time with a

smile. She thought about the long, fantastic life she had lived. She thought about Mitchell and Francine and their two incredible children, her best friends Joey and Annie.

~

The minivan sped through the airport parking lot. The weather was miserable, filled with torrential rain, clouds, and wind. The harsh reality of what the Keller family was about to face had not set in yet.

"What did the voicemail say, Fran?"

"That Zoey wasn't doing well. And that we needed to see her before it was too late."

Mr. Keller was at the wheel while Mrs. Keller sat in the passenger seat. Both twins, Annie and Joey, were fidgeting in the back. Their faces were distressed with confusion.

"What's going on, daddy?" asked Annie. She still wore her Minnie Mouse ears from the family vacation to Disneyland. Although the amazing trip ended yesterday, it already felt like it was forever ago. The agonizing plane ride this morning felt endless for Francine and Mitchell. They feared they wouldn't make it to Zoey in time.

"Nothing, sweetheart. We just need to get to the doggy place that's keeping Zoey."

"Is everything okay with her?" asked Joey.

Mr. Keller swerved a hard right onto the freeway. Everyone in the van lurched to the right before centering again. He was going well above the city speed limit.

"Mitch, you need to slow down."

"We don't have much time," responded Mitchell.

Mrs. Keller took out her phone. She tried to GPS the quickest route to the boarding facility. It dinged with a new set of directions.

"It says to take the next exit so we can bypass the traffic."

Mr. Keller made a puzzled face. "That doesn't make sense. Taking the next exit will put us west when we want to head east. It'll kill time; I'm keeping to the freeway."

"But Mitch, the directions say otherwise."

"I'm not listening to your phone," replied Mitchell. "Oh, crud, hang on."

The van swerved around a trailer truck that stopped short. Mr. Keller avoided the collision in the nick of time; the rain made visibility poor. He passed by the exit that his wife recommended taking. A minute later, a sizable glowing mass of car lights loomed ahead to a standstill. The traffic was impassable.

"I warned you!" yelled Mrs. Keller. "You should've listened to me."

"Did Zoey get hurt?" asked Annie.

"We're not sure. We're heading there now to see her."

"Is she going to be okay?" asked Joey.

Mr. Keller couldn't field questions and plot how to get out of the traffic. He grunted and boldly moved the van to the shoulder. The nervous father drove illegally down the stretch of grass as a series of angry honks sounded in his direction. He kept going until the next exit, then veered off from the freeway.

"What does the GPS say now?" asked Mr. Keller.

"Make a left," commanded Mrs. Keller.

The van skirted through the side streets. They were fifteen minutes out from the boarding facility. Both Joey and Annie exchanged glances of worry. They were scared something had happened to their dog, Zoey.

Another standstill of traffic. Neon-vested construction workers were holding the lane, allowing a slow cement truck to pass through. Again, Mr. Keller honked his horn with no success.

"I'm going to call the vet," said Mrs. Keller. She began ringing the number on speaker phone until Mr. Keller suggested making the call private.

"I wouldn't use the speaker phone," warned Mr. Keller.

Annie leaned forward with worry. "Why can't we hear, daddy?"

"Is Zoey dead?" asked Joey, his voice trembling.

"Just let mommy call the doctor," begged Mr. Keller.

The phone rang and rang, but the van remained motionless. They were helpless. Finally, a nurse answered the phone. Mrs. Keller informed the woman how traffic was horrendous.

"We are trying to get there, but it's near impossible. Can you give me an update on Zoey," asked Francine.

The children tried to listen in; they could hear someone's voice on the other end. Periodically, Francine would respond by saying, "Yes, I understand... Okay... Yes."

Joey couldn't take the mystery. He lashed out, "Mom, what the heck is the nurse saying?"

Mrs. Keller held her finger up to indicate she was getting answers.

"Well then, can I speak to Dr. Simmons?" asked Francine.

"Of course, hold on, please," responded the nurse.

Francine turned to Mitchell and said, "Find a way to get there faster."

"Mommy, what is wrong?" cried Annie. "What did the lady say?"

"The nurse said Zoey isn't doing the best, and she explained everything they are doing to improve her. And now I will ask Dr. Simmons about the next steps to take the dog home."

"Yes!" yelled Joey. "I knew she would be okay."

Mitchell looked at Francine from the corner of his eye, detecting his wife was telling the kids a white lie. Francine took a deep breath as she quickly glanced at Mitchell before looking at the battery life remaining on her phone. She was in the red with very little power left.

"Dang it, where is this doctor?" shouted Francine as she listened to the instrumental music playing on hold.

The traffic was about to end, and Mitchell was next in line to be called through by the construction worker managing the traffic.

A male voice was now on the phone. "Mrs. Keller, this is Dr. Simmons. I have some pretty troubling news to share with you."

His voice went quiet.

"Hello?" asked Francine. "Doctor, are you there?"

The line went dead. Her phone battery died.

"C'mon Francine, I told you to charge that thing before the flight."

"We'll use your phone," she responded.

"I am low on battery too, and I need mine for the GPS," said Mitchell.

"Daddy, the man is waving you up!"

Both kids pointed to the front of the traffic line. The workers allowed the remaining cars to move forward to the next street. Mr. Keller zipped into an outside lane, nearly hitting a motorcyclist. Annie and Joey both screamed.

The GPS told him to make a left in five miles. He had never taken this backroad, but directions showed a shortcut to the animal hospital. It would be seven minutes more.

Everyone in the car remained silent. It felt like seventy minutes instead of seven by the time Mr. Keller ripped into the parking lot. Once the vehicle was parked, the entire family ran into the building. They stood in the lobby, drenched from the rain. A cheery attendant named Ashleigh approached them.

"How can I help you, folks?"

"We're here about Zoey."

A grim look formed on her face. She avoided eye contact with the family. "Right, the Kellers. Let me go grab our doctor on call. He wanted to talk to you all in person."

A moment later, a veterinarian exited from the main

hall. It was Dr. Simmons. He, too, seemed distraught and saddened. He approached the family solemnly.

"I regret to inform you all that Zoey passed away early this morning."

A flood of heartbreak and sorrow consumed the Keller family. Both Joey and Annie started to cry. Mrs. Keller too.

Mr. Keller began to ask himself questions: *'How did this happen? How did she die? Was she sick?'*

But all the answers felt meaningless, and soon he slumped into the lobby chair in disbelief. His beloved Zoey was gone.

Chapter 1
A Promise Kept

The last day of school was extra special for Annie and Joey Keller, mainly because they had been waiting for this day for nearly a year. School was out, and summertime was starting, but their real excitement was tied to the report cards tucked in their backpacks. They only had a half-day of school, but it felt like an eternity waiting to be let out. When the final bell rang, the two siblings were eager to get home. There was a promise that was ready to be kept.

The yellow school bus screeched to a total halt at the stop sign. The double doors opened, welcoming a rush of the hot, humid air of the Carolinas. Annie and Joey said a quick goodbye to the bus driver and sprinted down the block towards their house, leaping onto the front porch.

Joey's report card nearly slipped out of his half-unzipped *Batman-and-Robin*-themed backpack. But he snatched it quickly and trailed behind Annie through the open screen doors. They were excited to show mom and dad the A's and B's they achieved in their classes.

Annie, the athlete of the duo, excelled in her sports and extracurricular clubs, such as Girl Scouts. She scored well in gym class, art, communications, and writing. Joey also shared a talent for writing, but his strong suits were mathematics, science, and history. As noted by his teachers, he was less talkative and shy compared to Annie. But they also noted his brilliance and love for reading comic books and novels above his grade level. So they found him equally impressive.

The twins worked especially hard this year for their grades. Because there was a possibility – *a reward of sorts* – waiting for them if they scored better grades than usual. The studying, homework dedication, and above-and-beyond effort to their scholastics would allow them to extend their family beyond just the two of them and their parents.

Their stellar, near-perfect report cards meant they were ready to adopt and care for two puppies. It had been a long time coming. Three years had passed since the family lost their dog, Zoey.

While Mr. and Mrs. Keller insisted it was best to put off adopting another pet after the loss of Zoey, Annie and Joey persisted. They vowed to care for two new puppies, tend to their every need, and never leave their side. They wanted to shower love on these puppies in the same manner their parents did for Zoey. They were also adamant it had to be two, that way, the dogs had each other to rely on.

The Keller parents finally relented to their kids' requests last autumn, but with conditions attached. First, Annie and Joey must continue to work their butts off to achieve excellent grades the entire school year, which would be their first at the local middle school.

Additionally, the two agreed to contribute more to chores around the house. They had no choice. Mrs. Keller worked as a teacher at the nearby high school, and Mr. Keller owned a popular hardware store in town -- the only one of its kind. This kept their parents constantly busy and overwhelmed.

To make extra money, Mrs. Keller took on tutoring sessions and taught the dozens of students she already had. Some nights she would come home with stacks of essays and assignments that needed to be graded, and then she would sign on to her computer for virtual tutor meetings. When she was done with it all, the kids would be in bed for the night.

Mr. Keller's shop was only run by him and Harold. But Harold was getting older and less enthusiastic about doing anything other than playing golf. This placed more work on Mr. Keller's shoulders. Simply put, adopting new pets would put even more weight on the Keller family's shoulders. If Annie and Joey wanted to be responsible as caregivers to two untrained puppies, they would have to prove it first.

The upgraded chores included mowing the lawn, cleaning the dishes, folding laundry, and painting the new tool shed in the backyard. At first, the two siblings slacked off in different areas, like Joey forgetting to unload the dishwasher or Annie rushing through painting the windowsills of the shed. But Annie and Joey fixed these simple mistakes and continued to put in the work, with both parents taking notice.

The star-studded report cards were the final icing on the cake. They held up their end of the promise and were dedicated to keeping up the hard work even after the adoption. To the kids, it was a no-brainer. They would do anything for the chance to have a family pet again. And this time, there would be two!

Annie and Joey raced to their mother's home office. The high school let out for summer two weeks ago, so Mrs. Keller was around a bit more to help Annie and Joey with their final exams. By the looks on her children's faces, she knew they had accomplished something big.

"Mom! Mom! Mom, take a look!"

The two siblings each took out their blue slips of paper, showcasing the highlighted grades and written remarks.

"Could today finally be the day?" asked Mrs. Keller with a wide smile.

She put on her reading glasses and examined the report cards for both Annie and Joey. Then, she read aloud the different teacher comments.

The comments from her teachers expressed that Annie is an outgoing student who is always the first to raise her hand and with confidence. She does not shy away from learning and displays sensational athletic skills but also practices excellent sportsmanship and leadership qualities. The teachers also wrote she made noticeable improvements in her writing skills and won the class award for the best painting in her art course: a portrait of her family dog, Zoey.

Mrs. Keller wiped a small tear from her eye at the last part, remembering the beauty of Annie's portrait. She did a fantastic job capturing Zoey's unique markings, shiny eyes, and snowy and amber colorations. The Kellers hung it next to another picture they created as a Christmas gift, a scene of all five of them huddled together.

She then read the teacher's comments on Joey's card. They describe him as a bright young boy who continues to excel. They mention his rankings in math and science are at the top of his class, and his proficiency in reading is simply fantastic. While somewhat shy in raising his hand and participating in class, Joey makes up for it with his strong vocabulary and impressive writing style. One teacher also notes he has excellent manners and is a great conversationalist when he opens up.

Joey blushed behind his rimmed glasses, whereas Annie's eyes lit up as her mother continued to note the excellencies on their report cards.

"Did we do it?" asked Annie with comical impatience. "Can we call dad? Did we keep the promise?"

Mrs. Keller chuckled at her daughter's insistence and dialed her husband's workshop number. She smiled at her two children.

"A promise kept is a promise kept," she said. "I think you two are ready for puppies."

Chapter 2
Like Brother Like Sister

"I didn't think you kids had it in you."

"Well, you were wrong, dad!"

Annie smiled gleefully at her father, who was driving the family minivan through their hometown. Sitting next to his sister in the backseat, Joey gave a nudge to her shoulder.

"Don't be rude, Annie, you'll blow it," egged Joey.

Mr. Keller and Mrs. Keller chuckled to themselves from the front seats of the van.

"I think you two can rest easy," assured Mrs. Keller. "It'll only be a few hours until our family of four grows to six."

The siblings smiled with jubilation. They had just finished a family lunch at the local cafe. Mr. Keller assigned Harold to watch over the store so the whole family could begin discussing the final plans for the adoption. They had to prep the house, assemble the doggy beds, and buy kibble and chew toys.

The Keller parents gave the kids some advice from when they adopted Zoey as a puppy and how stressful the first weeks were. But now, this would be two times the responsibility. Still, Annie and Joey remained confident throughout the whole lunch; they remained dedicated.

They were now on the way to a local pet store known for its wide selection of small dogs called Puppy Hub. The store had all kinds of breeds, both pure and mixed. Terriers, schnauzers, chihuahuas, and even pugs. But the Kellers hoped they would find two King Charles Cavaliers similar to Zoey.

Their quick drive to the store was suddenly slowed down as they reached the parking lot. A line of cars was backed up, each one trying to find a parking spot. A large banner hung in front of the pet store. It read: *PUPPY SALE TODAY!*

There was a long line of standing patrons composed of old and young couples and families large and small. They were all impatiently awaiting entry at the store.

It took a while to find a spot. Finally, the Keller family parked the minivan, which also served as Mr. Keller's work vehicle. Annie and Joey always had to climb over old, rusty tools. This time though, they did it without complaint. Their focus was getting to the line before it grew any longer. Their parents followed after the kids as the sweltering mid-afternoon sun soaked them with sweat. The estimated wait time was well over an hour, but Annie and Joey had no plans of abandoning their post.

Every ten minutes, people exited the store with a puppy or two in hand. A family of five left with four dachshunds! Two sisters went with three French bulldogs. Even the Kellers' old grumpy neighbor, Mrs. Stokes, adopted a chihuahua. It also did not take long for Annie and Joey to see some families and children leave with cavalier puppies in their arms, dismaying their hopes.

Finally, the Keller family's turn for entry arrived. The store was divided into sections based on different breeds of puppies. They were all brought in from across the state so that they would have the chance to find loving homes. An attendant at the front of the store greeted the Kellers.

"Welcome to Puppy Hub!" said the attendant. "How can we help you?"

"We were hoping to adopt two King Charles Cavaliers," answered Annie with excitement.

The older lady, whose name tag read Nelly, smiled and took out a photo from her wallet. It was a picture of a ruby-colored cavalier.

"This here used to be Kip," Nelly said proudly, pointing to the photograph. "He was my dog. He passed away last year. I loved him so much. Cavaliers are a special breed of dog. They will never stop loving you, young or old."

"We never stopped loving Zoey, our first dog. She died too," said Joey. "We'll love our new puppies so much."

Nelly smiled. "I think I know some puppies that would love you two very much, so follow me."

Annie and Joey's faces lit up with happiness, believing some cavaliers were still left. However, they were guided to Nelly's office instead of the puppy playroom area. She started searching for a pen and something to write on.

"My friend Arnold has a farm a few miles west of here," said Nelly, who began scribbling an address on a post-it note.

"His mama cavalier recently gave birth to a beautiful litter of puppies. They've had all their shots and vet exams and are ready to find new homes."

"Why adopt from this guy Arnold and not Puppy Hub?" asked Mr. Keller. "It's been quite the wait just to get in here."

Nelly only smiled more. "Arnold's cavaliers are special. Truly unique. I think they would be a great match for your family."

The comment radiated with the children. Before they knew it, they were back on the road and on their way to Arnold's farm.

~

The GPS said the ride would take twenty minutes, but it seemed like an hour for Annie and Joey. The winding roads and dirt trails leading to Arnold's farm felt like a zigzagging time loop. The area was very rural, layered with grassy plains and hayfields. Not many other homes were located this far from town.

They drove by a rickety barn with rotted wood boards. It was barely standing. A few yards from the barn was a dusty field with one decrepit scarecrow. Its straw face had a half smile, pecked away from neighboring crows.

"Looks like we're in the middle of nowhere," quipped Mr. Keller. "This looks like a scene from a horror film."

Mrs. Keller nodded in agreement. "Maybe we should just turn around, go home and start a new search."

"No!" shouted Annie and Joey. "Let's just stick to the plan."

"Fine," answered Mr. Keller. He reluctantly kept driving, passing by the creepy scarecrow and onto a new dirt trail. There was a marked sign with the written address matching the post-it note.

The ascent up the bumpy dirt driveway rattled the family minivan. Everyone grew quiet, silently questioning if the drive to Arnold's farm was a mistake.

Arnold, an elderly man in overall jeans, sat shirtless in a rocking chair on his wood porch. In his hand was a tin mug that hadn't been cleaned in decades. His straw hat fluttered in the wind but miraculously managed to stay in place on his head. Underneath the hat was a messy, stringy silver ponytail. His bushy white beard reminded Annie and Joey of Santa Claus, only it was much longer and downright scary looking.

"Okay, we're definitely in a horror movie," said Mr. Keller.

"You go up alone," demanded Mrs. Keller. "We'll stay in the car."

Mr. Keller parked the van and exited slowly as Arnold stood from the chair.

"How's it going?" asked Mr. Keller cautiously. "Are you Arnold?"

"Are you the Kellers?" asked Arnold, ignoring Mr. Keller's question.

"We are. I'm Mitchell. Nelly sent us. She said you'd be expecting our arrival."

"Of course," he confirmed. "I don't bite, and neither do the dogs here. Your family can come out of the van now."

Mrs. Keller and the kids exited the minivan, recognizing Arnold was just a friendly old man.

"This is my wife Francine, and these are my kids, Annie and Joey. How do you know Nelly?"

"Nelly used to be my neighbor," answered Arnold softly. "But then she moved closer to town. She was my wife's best friend before her passing."

The Kellers gave their condolences. Arnold thanked them.

"My wife passed away a few months ago. She and I have been housing, fostering, and providing cavaliers for generations," he said solemnly. "When she died, our mama and papa cavaliers – Queen and Chaser – were expecting. The puppies they gave birth to are the last of their final litter. Queen is getting old, as is Chaser. As am I. This litter has a special place in my heart."

The Kellers followed Arnold as he led them through the old house to the backyard area. The cavalier parents, a tricolor female and a Blenheim male, were nestled away in the corner of a fenced playpen. Two puppies were burrowed comfortably in between the adult dogs.

"This last litter originally had eight puppies," said Arnold. "Nelly helped me find a home for six of them. There are two left, a brother and a sister. I've held on to them for as long as I could. Not sure how to explain it, but these two are truly special. When Nelly called me today saying two amazing kids, a brother and a sister, wanted to adopt them, I wanted to resist. But I knew it was time to let them go into the care of someone else."

"What makes them so special?" asked Annie.

"Their bond," answered Arnold. "These two pups have a sibling bond like no other. They're truly inseparable. I don't think I could let someone adopt one without the other. It's a bond I can't explain, but it's born out of love."

The two little puppies awakened from the nap under their mother's belly. They stretched and yawned with all their might. Their tails wagged simultaneously as they took notice of the strange human visitors.

Annie's eyes lit up, as did Joey's. The puppies were so small and fragile, yet so happy and wide-eyed. The brother was a tricolor of black, white, and brown, just like his mother, Queen. The sister, a Blenheim, resembled the father, Chaser, with a coat coloring of chestnut and vanilla.

"They are both healthy and vaccinated," said Arnold.

Mitchell asked, "Is there anything we need to know?"

"To be fully transparent, the vet detected a hint of cloudiness in the female's right eye. It may impact her vision later on, but it won't be too severe if it does," confirmed the old farmer.

"I would never give away puppies if I didn't think they would be okay and in good hands," added Arnold.

"Can we hold them?" Annie asked.

Arnold nodded, allowing her and Joey to hold the pups.

The puppies instantly gravitated to the two children. Their dinky frames were coated with fluffy hair and big curious eyes. They licked the faces of the Keller kids, demonstrating their limitless affection. The sister pup snuggled into

Annie's arms while the brother pup plopped himself onto Joey's crisscrossed lap.

Arnold seemed pleased by how quick the pups attached themselves to the kids. It did not take long for Mr. and Mrs. Keller to instantly fall in love with the puppies.

"The one in Annie's arms reminds me of Zoey," said Mrs. Keller thoughtfully.

Arnold took a seat next to Annie. "What would you name this little one?"

Annie thought for a moment while she examined the adorable, plump puppy. Her beady eyes gazed back at Annie in wonder. The golden markings of chestnut fur reminded Annie of all things light and vibrant.

"I think I would name her Summer," said Annie confidently, hugging her closely. "It's my favorite season. It's when I'm happiest – like right now."

Annie and her pup snuggled their noses. Then, the little doggy, now named Summer, let out a sneeze.

"You two will get along very well," Annie joked to Joey.

Arnold turned his attention to the boy. "And what would you name that crazy fella? Winter, I suppose?"

Joey shook his head. "I don't really like the winter season."

"Fair enough. Perhaps name him after something you do enjoy?"

Joey thought about it for a moment. He did not mind the name Winter, but he wanted something more meaningful. He stared at his pup, who stared back, almost unblinking.

His posture was stoic and valiant. This was a puppy ready for anything. He stood prepared to take action with his new sidekick, Joey.

Joey then thought about his Batman and Robin comic books. Reading them on the bus to and from school, in his bedroom while doing homework, and underneath the bed-sheets with his camp flashlight when he was supposed to be sleeping. The stories they told were always action-packed.

"My favorite superhero is Batman's sidekick, Robin," Joey finally answered. "I think his name should be Robin."

"His face looks like he's wearing a mask," pointed out Mrs. Keller, highlighting the puppy's facial markings.

"I think it's fitting," affirmed Mr. Keller.

Arnold smiled as he handed the Keller family their new puppies, Robin and Summer.

As the Keller family drove away, Annie commented that Arnold was very nice. Joey agreed too.

"This is why you can't judge a book by its cover," said Mrs. Keller. "Imagine if we ended up turning around and leaving."

"I'm glad we didn't," said Annie. "This is the best day of our lives."

Chapter 3
Getting Started with Robin & Summer

The first two weeks with the puppies were tough. Both would have accidents. Summer once peed in Mrs. Keller's home office, and Robin peed in his crate out of anxiousness during a trip to the vet. They were messy eating their kibble, sometimes spilling pellets across the kitchen floor. And the teething had been out of control. The pups chewed on everything, including pencils, books, curtains, chair legs, backpack straps, and shoes. They even chewed on some of their dad's tools that were lying around.

But after those first two weeks, the chaos eased, and the fun began. The dogs started listening. The Keller kids were on their A-game, much like their report cards, and were training the dogs constantly and responsibly.

By the end of the second month, Robin and Summer were on their way to being great pets and treasured members of the Keller family.

Like clockwork, Annie and Joey played fetch with the pups each day after their training sessions. This included teaching the dogs proper walking routines and following commands of *sit* and *stay*.

In late August, the Kellers loaded up a rented Winnebago and took the puppies on a two-week road trip to multiple RV parks. After what happened to Zoey, the Keller kids insisted that any family vacations included the puppies too. This meant the family would skip vacations to places like

Disneyland, which the kids were more than okay with. The pups were still young, but neither Keller wanted to take a chance with a boarding facility.

On the trip, Robin and Summer were shown the natural landscapes of the Carolinas, consisting of open fields, dense woodlands, and crystal-clear lakes. Whenever they stopped for the day, Annie and Joey would prepare the leashes – a pink one for Summer, a red one for Robin – and take the dogs for a walk around the rows of RVs. They met other dogs of all shapes and sizes and different species of pets, such as a neighboring tabby cat and a white-bellied parrot.

The dogs behaved well, even in close quarters together. Though the two pups come from the same litter and share similar traits, they were also different in their behaviorisms.

Robin became the quicksilver of the duo. His hind legs were lengthy for his frame, but they allowed him to dash like his father Chaser at lightning-fast speeds. He also could jump and leap higher than a typical cavalier. Mrs. Keller would joke that he was part cat. On walks, Robin would zig and zag in every direction. He was impossible to slow down; he would run for miles if it were not for the leash restraint.

Similarly to his physical speed, Robin proved to be a brilliant dog. His sense of smell and hearing were precise, but this could sometimes be difficult to taper down. He was always on the hunt and wanted to be on the go. It took Joey reading his comic books aloud to curb Robin's hyper-behavior.

Robin would always be the first to scoop and snatch the ball during fetch. Often, however, he was not the returnee. That would be Summer.

She was less speedy and not as skillful in jumps and leaps. But she behaved well with verbal commands, often listening better than Robin. And as Arnold warned, Summer's right eye was doughy. This led her to have minor stifles in vision and coordination compared to her brother.

But Summer was strong. Very strong. She outweighed Robin by build and could snatch any toy or item out of his jaws. Robin's barking was squawky, but Summer's bark held thunderous attention. If she barked, it meant business. Robin might be the brains, but Summer was ultimately the muscle.

Summer also had better skills in remaining calm than Robin and less separation anxiety. Overall, she displayed better independence. While Robin needed to be in the same room as Joey nonstop, Summer was balanced with her time. Some nights she would sleep with Annie, but other nights she was content staying in her doggy bed.

Fetch had turned into an actual 50/50 guessing game about who would return the ball first. However, Robin's speed and quickness allowed him to succeed every time in the first few weeks.

Eventually, Summer got bolder. She realized she could beat her brother in the tug-o-war battle and quickly snatched the ball back.

The battle between the siblings became entertaining to watch. At times, Robin would manage to evade Summer and return the ball. But then, other times, Summer pulled the ball away from Robin and returned it herself. No matter who won, Summer always attempted to use her rear end as a weapon. The Kellers would be hysterically laughing as she tried to bully Robin with her butt.

It reached a point where the Keller family started making bets. Mrs. Keller would bet on Robin, but Mr. Keller saw more promise in Summer's alpha aggression and strength. And as for the kids, they always stayed true to their allegiances. Annie for Summer, and Joey for Robin.

As time went on, their bond became stronger, but so did their competitive nature. A perfect example is the game of fetch that occurred on Labor Day Weekend. Joey initiated the game by tossing a ball as far away as possible. Both dogs were in a heated race to win the game. But Summer barreled into Robin with her butt, knocking him over. She then snatched up the ball and proudly strode back to the awaiting family.

Robin would not give up. He zipped past Summer's left side. She tried to barricade him with her butt and tail, but he was too fast. He went for the ball, managing to snag its free side.

In unison, the two puppies, each clutching a side of the tennis ball, sprinted back to the Kellers. Simultaneously, they dropped the ball at their feet. A tie between the two became a common theme in the past week. They wagged their tails rapidly, waiting for the rewards.

"Alright, give them both treats; It's a draw," Mr. Keller relented.

Both Annie and Joey fed their respective dogs a peanut butter biscuit. The pups hastily gobbled the treats. Summer slumped her body by Annie's side, who was sitting on the porch. Robin joined in on the cuddle, and Joey placed a water bowl in front of the two. They had been playing fetch for over an hour; the dogs were worn out.

"These rascals are going to miss the games when you two head back to school," said Mrs. Keller.

"Don't remind us, mom," said Annie, jokingly plugging her earlobes to drown out the word *school*.

Only a few days were left until Annie and Joey returned for the fall semester. They reaffirmed the promise to their parents to keep their grades strong and to participate in class discussions. But they also promised to continue their responsibilities of chores and housework. This meant less time spent with Summer and Robin.

The evening sunset neared completion. The Keller parents went back inside the house while the Keller kids remained outside with the dogs, cuddling together. They glanced up at the moon, distant and away in the darkening sky, like a silver coin. Annie could sense worry on Joey's face as the puppies napped and lightly snored.

"What's wrong, Joey?"

Joey sighed. "When we return to school, mom and dad will be at work. I'm just worried Robin and Summer will feel lonely."

Hearing his name, Robin perked his head up, tilting his face back and forth as if attempting to understand the conversation. Summer continued her nasal snoring.

"They have each other, Joey," reassured Annie. She patted Robin's noggin. "I'm just bummed we'll be spending less time with them until next summer vacation."

Annie then picked up the tennis ball, which sparked both dogs' attention. They arched their backs and stretched their ligaments, but kept their eyes glazed and glued to the fuzzy object.

"I say we make every second count while we still can," she added.

Joey grinned in agreement. Annie winded her arm up for the pitch and rocketed the ball across the yard.

Robin bolted for the ball, and Summer chased after him. They repeatedly played fetch as the night sky blossomed, cherishing and soaking up every last minute of fun they could get out of their best friends. They were blissfully unaware that their time together would soon be less frequent.

Mr. and Mrs. Keller watched the extended game of fetch from the kitchen window. They were cleaning dishes together when Mr. Keller suggested, "Shouldn't we call the kids in soon? They're probably going to need a shower before bedtime."

Mrs. Keller shook her head and smiled. "No. Let them play. This is one of those memories we will all cherish forever."

Chapter 4
Housebound

Routinely, Annie and Joey would wake up early before school. It was not easy to do. Autumn mornings were a little colder than usual in the Carolinas this year. Annie and Joey went from dressing in shorts and t-shirts to corduroys and sweatshirts. But the early morning was the only time they had to interact with Robin and Summer before a daunting schedule of classes, sports, clubs, and homework.

By late fall, it was apparent the upcoming winter would be numbing and chilly. The Carolinas would feel as cold as Canada.

With each passing day, the daylight hours receded. And as the temperatures dropped, the kids spent a little less time each morning with the dogs. The mornings were staying dark longer. The sun didn't say hello until around 7 o'clock. Before school, activities outside the house, such as neighborhood walks and playing fetch, were no longer options. Even weekends were out of the question; it was too cold. Playtime became obsolete by the Thanksgiving holiday.

It saddened Robin and Summer that this was their new reality. Even on days when the weather was less than brutal, Annie and Joey were busy from morning to night. Mrs. Keller was occupied teaching and tutoring her high school students. Mr. Keller worked around the clock at the hardware store after his only employee, Harold, finally decided to retire. And to make matters worse, financial strains were weighing down on Mitchell's shoulders. The economy started to weaken months earlier, the forecast was worsening, and sales at the store were terrible.

The situation became where Mr. Keller was never around. He would only return to the house at lunchtime for ten minutes to quickly feed and let the dogs out.

The Keller family was not firing on all cylinders, so the dogs paid a high price. For most days of the week, Robin and Summer were home alone. As a result, they became lethargic and arguably depressed.

Luckily, the misery showed signs of ending by the end of December; Summer and Robin were rewarded with attention and love during the Christmas holiday.

All the Kellers were under one roof, cozying together as the weather deepened into the single digits at night. Robin would curl up into a ball on Joey's lap, nestling into his blanket. Summer would snuggle with Annie by the fireplace, admiring the glowing, orange-brightened embers crackling off the wood. The fire would cast a beautiful reflection off Summer's beady, dark eyes. The moment was warm, inviting, and fleeting.

Christmas came and went. Annie and Joey returned to their busy routines when school returned to session after New Year's Day. The dogs fell back into the mundane loneliness of the Keller household.

By February, the workload piled up for Annie and Joey. Midterm exams, after-school clubs, sports, and extra credit community service hours took up all their time. Some mornings the kids were so tired they wouldn't even acknowledge the dogs before leaving for school. And by the time they returned home, they had dinner, a bath, and lights out.

Nights of the bitter cold soon transitioned into a season of blossoming cherry trees and lilac bushes. It was beautiful again. Mrs. Keller would sing, "Spring has finally sprung."

Regardless, the dogs were still forgotten for most hours of the day. They would sit by the glass sliding doors leading to the backyard. For hours they'd do nothing but watch the sun journey across the greening landscape. The short lunch visits by Mr. Keller were their only escape from the house. Ten minutes of fresh air wasn't enough, but Summer and Robin made every second count. They would chase squirrels, roll in the grass, and dig small holes.

The dog's bond with the Keller kids continued to strain.

The twins had started forgetting to keep their promises to their parents. Annie's focus needed sharpening at school, with teachers reporting she was becoming the class clown. As a result, her grades started to slip. This did not make the Keller parents happy. If Annie tried to chill out and watch TV or play around with Summer instead of doing homework, her mother would stop it all.

"Get back to the books," Mrs. Keller would demand.

Joey made things even more cumbersome with his reclusive behavior. He had become too attached to video games, Mr. Keller had determined. Joey even abandoned reading his comic books. Instead of reading about Batman, the young boy's eyes would be glued to the computer screen.

His eyes would grow bloodshot, and his fingers would numb, trying to work his way up to the next level of each game he played.

Joey became totally unaware of his surroundings. For example, Mr. Keller had a rare opportunity to close the store early because of a power outage that shut down the entire strip mall where his store was located. It was two o'clock on a Saturday afternoon when he arrived home to find Robin scratching feverishly on Joey's bedroom door.

Mr. Keller yelled up the stairs, "Joey, the dog has to go out; what are you doing?"

Mitchell received no answer. Upset, he opened Joey's door without knocking. His son had headphones on. He was totally engrossed in a video game.

"Son, I called your name. Robin is begging to go out to the bathroom. Turn off that game now; give yourself a break. Take the dogs for a walk; the weather is decent right now."

"In a minute, dad, I can't exit out of my game right now!"

Too tired to argue, Mr. Keller leashed up the dogs for a rare walk. It was during the stroll that Mitchell realized he and Francine needed to have a long talk.

Later that night, while lying in bed, Mr. Keller said to Mrs. Keller: "What Joey is doing is unhealthy, Francine. We have to do something!"

"I agree," she responded.

The following day the Keller parents took away the gaming console. They told Joey it was for his own good.

Francine and Mitchell hoped this would prompt Joey to be more active, outgoing, and healthy.

Sadly, it did nothing but upset Joey further. At least twice or thrice a week, the Keller parents would receive a call from the school nurse saying Joey reported feeling ill. Each time it was something new bothering him. It was a constant charade of crying wolf and an attempt to go home and play video games.

For the Keller kids, the school year did not finish strong or pleasant. Joey's situation showed no improvement, and Annie focused less on school and sports than in years past. Instead, she was more interested in gossiping about boys with her clique of friends.

With summer approaching, the Keller parents tossed ideas to redirect Annie and Joey's focus. Neither of the kids was old enough to be working jobs, and house chores weren't enough.

Mr. and Mrs. Keller recognized they, too, fell short. They were too busy working their jobs; they needed to spend more time with the kids. But how could they? Francine had taken on more tutoring sessions to help Mitchell with expenses at home. And in addition to administering end-of-year exams at the high school, Francine was unexpectedly approached by her principal to lead the summer school courses for those who failed. To Mrs. Keller, it felt more like a burden than a promotion. It didn't help that Mr. Keller still hadn't found a replacement for Harold at the store.

"People just don't want to work anymore," Mr. Keller had relented one night to his wife. "Francine, it makes me worried about our kids and their future. They need better discipline. The kids need to reignite the passion they had when they were all revved up about adopting the dogs."

"I agree," said Mrs. Keller.

"And some big family vacation won't cut it this year," he continued. "We're stretched thin with our time as it is, and financially we can't afford to skip work. So we can't be heading out of town doing something big like the RV trip from last summer."

Francine responded, "But I don't want the kids just withering away in their rooms this summer; they need to *do something*."

Mr. Keller asked, "What do we do?"

Francine answered, "I think I have an idea."

~

On the Sunday before the last week of school, the Keller parents made an announcement to their children. Annie and Joey would be leaving in two weeks for sleepaway camp for the summer. The Wilderness World Camp, specifically. It was the same camp Francine had gone to when she was a kid. Her cousin Missy was the camp's founding partner, so all family members were given lifetime discounts. Francine avoided sending the kids in years past because she didn't like the idea of paying less than other families, but this year was a must.

The kids did not take the news well, especially Joey. Annie did not want to be away from her friends. Joey hated the idea of not being close to an internet connection. The Keller parents insisted they relearn the values they forgot about after adopting the dogs. But nobody was more devastated by the news than Robin and Summer.

Everyone went to bed a little bit sad that night. Summer went to cuddle with Annie, but she was not in the mood to be bothered. Surprisingly, a somber Joey gave Robin the boot too. The dogs resorted to the living room. Once again, they were alone. The two dogs snuggled together, but their eyes remained open. Both dogs wondered what the next few weeks without Annie and Joey would feel like. They hoped it was far from the feelings of loneliness and abandonment that fueled their winter.

Chapter 5
The Long Trip Ahead

The Keller parents hastily planned a last-minute trip to their children's sleepaway camp. The kids had two weeks remaining, and they were doing very well. They called every night, talking about the team-building activities they had achieved that day. Every week, the Keller parents would receive dozens of emailed pictures. Joey and Annie would be swimming in the lake, riding bikes, hiking trails, pitching tents, and even ziplining!

In the emails, they wrote about the skills they learned, such as starting a campfire, tending to gardens, and engaging in teamwork. One emailed picture had the two of them posing with the camp owner's dog, Boomer, the western terrier.

The kids were thriving.

But late last night, Mrs. Keller received a call from Wilderness World Camp director, Edwin Gavan, saying Joey had fallen and gotten hurt. And this time, he was not crying wolf. He fell from a rock climbing scaffold and broke his wrist. The camp's medic, Martha, took him to the nearest hospital, where he received an arm cast.

Joey sounded sad on the phone. He was definitely disheveled. There was not much he could do at the camp with a broken wrist. Unfortunately, he was going to have to return home.

Annie wanted to stay, but she recognized it would be

silly for her parents to drive up north again a few weeks later when the camp was scheduled to end. It would put unnecessary pressure on her parents to take off from work a second time, which wasn't an option. Like her brother, she was also starting to miss Robin and Summer.

"Can you bring the dogs when you come to get us? I miss them so much," said Joey with sorrow in his voice.

"Me too," added Annie. "They went on our RV trip last summer. I'm sure they can handle a six-hour car ride."

Mr. Keller protested, claiming it would be easier if Mrs. Stokes watched over the dogs. But the kids pushed back. It had been almost an entire month since they saw Robin and Summer. Plus, they wanted to make up for their poor behavior over the winter and spring. They recognized they weren't as responsible and caring with Summer and Robin as they had promised.

And then there was the kids' fear of leaving the dogs behind. It was a bad omen, a reminder of what happened with Zoey. Their dad couldn't protest against those feelings.

It was a sunny, blistering hot morning. Mitchell and Francine were ready to leave for Wilderness World Camp.

"Mitchell, are you kidding me? How will we fit my suitcase and the dog carrier with all these boxes?"

"Francine, I cannot unload these boxes by myself. So if you want to delay the trip and head to the store, great. You can help me unload eight boxes of paint cans and brushes for the store shelves before we go."

"Why did you buy so many paint boxes?" asked Francine.

"Last year, we saw a huge uptick in people buying paint for end-of-summer projects, so I thought it would be best to have more in stock," responded Mitchell.

Mr. Keller, sweating through his t-shirt, hurled his body weight into his wife's overstuffed suitcase. It would not fit with all the boxes in the way. All of it together hindered the minivan's hatch from closing shut. He gave it another shove, then another. Finally, there was some wiggle room, with only a section of space left unoccupied.

"Pass me the dog carrier, would you please?" asked Mr. Keller. "Unless you have another overpacked suitcase that needs to be stuffed in here."

Mrs. Keller rolled her eyes. "Are you kidding, I packed all of your clothes and mine together, plus I added a few changes of shorts and shirts for the kids. And in the front zipper, I packed the dog food, medicine, and toys."

"Once again, you overpacked," scolded Mitchell.

"I know you're cranky, but can you curb your nasty tone of voice Mitch?"

"I'm not cranky. I'm tired of working my butt off and getting criticized as a result," said Mr. Keller. "How about we switch jobs? You run the store for a week, which means you can move the boxes of paint onto the shelves while I sit on the sofa and grade math papers."

Francine purposely ignored his snarky remarks and reminded Mitchell not to forget the carrier containing Robin and Summer.

"Be careful, Mitch, don't throw your back out lifting the dogs," warned Francine.

"I'm sure they're no heavier than eight boxes filled with Benjamin Moore. I think I'll be okay with the lift, but thanks for the concern," replied Mitchell with sarcasm.

The dogs had gained a couple pounds since they last traveled, but Mr. Keller could place it gently into the remaining open space.

He started the car, adjusted his rearview mirror, and blasted the air conditioning to its maximum level. The temperature outside was a scorching ninety-eight degrees.

It was essential to keep hydrated too. Mrs. Keller filled up a water bowl and placed it next to the carrier. She unzipped the mesh window for the dogs to peek their heads through. Robin gulped for the water first, then Summer wiggled her way to the bowl. They commenced a back-and-forth rhythm of taking turns drinking the water. The bowl was half empty by the time they were finished, and the drive hadn't even started.

"They'll need to pee soon," quipped Mr. Keller. "Which means we'll have to stop sooner than I want to."

"You're always in need of a bathroom break yourself," Mrs. Keller quipped back.

They had a six-hour drive ahead of them. They hoped to reach the campgrounds before dusk and check in at a hotel without issue.

The back door to the minivan closed as the dogs positioned themselves into nap mode. Their understanding of what was going on was limited. Still, they recognized the scent of Annie and Joey's clothes from the suitcase. They knew they would be traveling to see them and dreamt of reuniting with their favorite two people. They just had to sit tight for the long trip ahead.

~

Cluh-clunk.

Robin jolted awake first, which stirred Summer too. The van had pulled into a general store's gas station lot. The GPS on Mr. Keller's dashboard said they were an hour away from the campground location. The dogs had slept most of the car ride, though they woke a few times from the loudness of Mr. Keller's sports podcast on the old minivan's speakers.

"I'll start the pump, but you have to keep an eye on it; I need to use the restroom," said Mr. Keller, unbuckling his seatbelt. "I'll be quick."

"I can take care of the pump," retorted Mrs. Keller. "I'll take the dogs for a potty break, too, while we fill up."

"Want anything from the store?"

"I'll take green tea and aspirin. I have a headache from being forced to listen to your podcast."

Mr. Keller made way for the store while Mrs. Keller leashed up Robin and Summer. The pups were amped to be let out of the cramped van. Plus, they needed to tinkle terribly.

She placed the gasoline spout in the minivan's fuel port and turned on the automatic pump. It continued pumping while she walked the dogs over to the rest area. The feeling of the hot sun after hours of ventilated air conditioning was a noticeable contrast for both the dogs and Mrs. Keller. She stretched her legs and back while Robin and Summer sniffed and toiled around until they finally settled at a grassy patch near a cedar tree to relieve themselves.

A tiny thump was felt by Robin on the top of his head. He looked up to see a pesky squirrel chewing on a tree nut. Then the squirrel discarded that nut too, and it fell and thumped Robin's head again. He barked, then Summer did too. Mrs. Keller shooed the dogs to be quiet. Summer listened, and she immediately lost interest in the squirrel. But Robin's eyes remained fixated on the devious gray creature who slyly stared back from the high branches.

"Good job, pups," complimented Mrs. Keller, guiding them back to the minivan. Robin resisted slightly, wanting to confront the squirrel but relented and followed Mrs. Keller and Summer.

Mrs. Keller removed the leashes and placed Robin, then Summer, back into the carrier. She softly repositioned the blankets and dog toys around them.

Her fixing the carrier was interrupted by what sounded like guzzling water. But it wasn't water; it was gasoline! The pump fell from the port and was now spilling gas all over the cement and onto the minivan.

"Dang it!"

Mrs. Keller ran over to stop the leak. Some of the gasoline dripped on her pants, which she tried to wipe off. In a matter of seconds, Mrs. Keller was in a messy situation. One that was quite distracting.

Summer's attention was drawn to Mrs. Keller's

mishap, as was Robin's. But Robin quickly turned back to the cedar tree yards ahead. The squirrel appeared at the base of the tree, searching for more nuts. Soon, two more squirrels joined him, and then another. Robin began wagging his tail and pawed at the carrier wall.

The mesh door was unzipped. The side of the carrier was left open. Domestic instinct told him to stay put, but his primal instinct told him to chase after the squirrel.

Robin dashed out of the carrier like a bolt of lightning. Summer, unsure of her brother's intentions, chased after him. The squirrels panicked. While most of them went back up the tree, the devious one ran across the field, tempting Robin to continue his pursuit. Summer trailed behind. They were out of earshot of Mrs. Keller, who had just finished fixing the leaky pump.

"You alright, Francine?"

Mr. Keller approached her from the general store exit, holding a bag of food and drink items. He wanted to make a jaded joke about the spilled gasoline on his minivan, but he refrained. Nevertheless, the situation had his wife visibly distressed.

"No, I'm not; my pants are ruined, and I smell like gasoline," she answered, staring at her stained pants.

"So what do you want to do?"

"I just want to get to Joey. And Annie. It's just stressful when things like this happen. I wish we didn't stop," said Mrs. Keller.

Mr. Keller felt terrible for his wife, but there was

nothing he could do. He passed her green tea and moved quickly to get back into the minivan.

They entered their respective seats and buckled up. The hatch was still open, so Mr. Keller clicked the button for the automatic close. He could see the outline of the carrier from his rearview mirror, camouflaged with piled-on blankets and toys.

Trying to lighten the tense situation, Mr. Keller made a small joke.

"No need to call and alert the kids that we're almost there. They can probably smell your pants from here."

Mrs. Keller offered no reply. She kept her head down, focusing entirely on the stains she was trying to scrub off with cleaning wipes.

Mr. Keller turned his focus on resetting the GPS and putting his podcast back on, then drove out of the station lot and merged back onto the highway. Meanwhile, Robin abandoned his pursuit of the squirrel and returned to the cedar tree. He could see Summer was heading back to the station lot, frantically sniffing around for the whereabouts of the disappeared parents.

Chapter 6
Highway of Danger

Zooooooom, zoom.

The Kellers were nowhere. No humans were around. Robin and Summer were alone and confused, with only the sounds of passing cars. Maybe the Keller parents would come back, they wondered. But with each passing second, the chance the Kellers would return grew slim. The dogs could feel it in their guts.

Robin had joined Summer in her frantic search. They circled the gas station three times. Finally, they checked by the pumps, sniffing up the pungent smells of gasoline. Still, their search became useless.

Tired of searching, the puppies then rested in the grass patch. They were hoping for a miracle. Five minutes passed, then ten. Robin wanted to resume searching, but Summer opted to stay put. They were at a crossroads of confusion. How could they be left behind by the people they love? Something just wasn't right.

Zooooooom.

The dogs became fixated on cars speeding along the interstate. None of them looked like the Keller family minivan. Summer and Robin didn't know where to turn. There was very little space to wander around the gas station. The only place to hang out was along the strip of grass by the cedar tree.

Growing antsy, Robin circled the tree in search of the

mischievous squirrels. There was no sign of them, but Robin caught the scent of their presence. He then heard Summer bark. She was now standing by the parking lot entrance. He ran over to see what she had spotted. It was a flurry of four squirrels preparing to cross the busy highway.

Robin and Summer barked at the squirrels, forcing them to dart out. The devious squirrel from before, identifiable by his larger size and ratty tail, trailed behind the other three. He was carrying a tree nut too large for its mouth.

Two of the squirrels dashed quickly and made it across with no issue, entering the shrubberies and bushes of an expansive forest. The third squirrel lagged behind and came close to meeting its end under the tire of an eighteen-wheeler. It then scurried quickly to safety, waiting for the ratty-tailed squirrel to finish its crossing.

The last squirrel – *the devious, ratty-tailed squirrel* – made it past the southbound side of the highway. But as he scurried over the two painted yellow lines, the tree nut accidentally dropped from his mouth. It lay in the center of the northbound road.

Greedily, the squirrel tried retrieving the nut. But the creature was moving slowly. The sizzling hot pavement cooked by the afternoon sun was hurting his feet. He had trouble snatching the nut up. It, too, was hot. It burned his mouth. Ultimately, his efforts were futile.

Robin and Summer, eyes wide and frightened, looked away in horror as an eighteen-wheeler chugged toward the shell-shocked, ratty-tailed squirrel. The trucker blasted his horn, but it was too late to swerve away. Mere seconds later, the squirrel was nothing more than roadkill.

The other squirrels quickly recognized and accepted the loss of their comrade and moved on. They headed into the forest.

Robin had a feeling. It was an intuition. He thought the forest was where they had to go if they wanted to find the Kellers. Summer was not crazy about the idea, but she accepted the path. If they were to reunite with Francine and Mitchell, they would need to tap into their survival instincts.

Summer and Robin looked each way before crossing the highway. From left to right, then back to the left. No cars, no trucks. This appeared to be their clearing. As Robin placed a paw on the road, feeling the radiating warmth of the cement, an SUV passed by on the northbound lane. Then a motorcade of motorcycles appeared in the southbound section. A sedan followed, honking loudly at the frightened pups.

The visuals and sounds reminded Robin of the video game *Frogger,* which Joey often played. The goal was to get the frog across a section of roads, with cars coming from every direction. Joey wasn't very good at the game; there were plenty of times his frog avatar would die by the computerized vehicles.

Robin retracted his paw in fear. He and Summer were in a real-life *Frogger* situation. But, unlike the video game, there were no do-overs or retries. If they were going to cross, they would have to do it in one try. And fast. No hesitations.

The dogs did another left-right-left check and then ran for their lives.

Robin, always the fast one, sped ahead of Summer. No cars passed by in the southbound lane. They continued to sprint. But then Robin froze as he saw the corpse of the ratty-tailed squirrel. Its mangled body stunned him into stillness. It was too unnerving for the young pup.

The deafening sound of a large vehicle could be heard, roaring its way on the northbound road. The unmistakable *vroom* drew closer and closer, but Robin was too shaken to notice.

Summer acted fast. She caught up to her brother and tugged on his collar to move forward. She managed to lead him into finishing the crossing. But they were running low on time; more cars were coming in by the second.

The beeping horn sound came in two short bursts, startling both dogs. A fast-moving USPS truck was in sight. The pups knew they had to escape the final lane of the interstate. They leaped from the road and fell down the ravine – tumbling into a muddy grove. Three seconds later, the truck whizzed past the two disheveled pups.

Robin and Summer regained composure, priding themselves on accomplishing the dangerous feat. But as they looked around their surroundings – *sprawling dense trees, endless dirt trails, strange noises of wildlife and woodland creatures* – they realized their perilous journey back to the Kellers was just beginning.

Chapter 7
Big Mistake

"Can we turn off the podcast for a little while?"

Mrs. Keller continued to rub the gasoline stain out of her pants. She tried using more cleaning wipes from her purse. No luck. What also did not help was Mr. Keller streaming his loud sports podcast through the minivan speakers. The host kept ranting about the trade of a famous football player.

"How can I turn this off when my favorite quarterback is headed to Tampa Bay?" asked Mr. Keller in disbelief.

"Trust me, I think you'll live," Mrs. Keller retorted while scrubbing the stain.

Mr. Keller killed the radio. It had been twenty minutes since they left the gas station. The minivan was quiet, except for Mrs. Keller cleaning her pants.

"Actually, you're right," said Mr. Keller. "The silence is pleasant."

Mrs. Keller stopped scrubbing and felt a wave of suspicion overcome her. A bad feeling sat in the pit of her stomach.

"It's almost too quiet," she said.

She then turned toward the back of the van. She could see the outline of the carrier, but it was blocked by the rear seats and clutter of boxes.

"Robin? Summer?" asked Mrs. Keller aloud.

No answer.

"They're just sleeping," assured Mr. Keller.

The van hit a pothole. Not a stir, muffle, or bark arose from the back of the minivan.

"Pull over," she demanded.

"We're almost there; why don't we wait?"

Francine yelled, "Just please pull over. Quickly."

Mr. Keller flicked on his hazard lights and brought the van to the shoulder of the highway. He started to suspect something amiss too.

Without hesitation, Mrs. Keller unbuckled her seatbelt and raced to the back. She opened the hatch door, revealing her fear as a stark reality.

The carrier was empty. The dogs were gone.

Mr. Keller quickly left his seat after hearing his wife's gasp. For the sake of panic, he checked behind the luggage, boxes, and under the blankets. He discovered the unzipped side door of the carrier.

"Oh no. Oh no! No… "

Mrs. Keller repeatedly denied what she knew to be true. The dogs were missing.

"I should have double-checked the carrier! They must be back at the gas station," claimed Francine.

Sweat from the summer heat and excessive worry formed on Mr. Keller's brow. Both parents stood silent for a second, not sure what to say.

"Someone there must better have found them," said Mr. Keller.

Francine responded, "Or maybe someone took them. They are cavaliers, for Heaven's sake."

"Let's not get ahead of ourselves. Let's stay calm. But dang it, Fran, I can't believe you forgot to check the carrier! What the heck were you thinking?"

Tears were streaming down Mrs. Keller's cheeks. She felt immense guilt and sorrow. But her husband's comment sent her into a state of anger.

"You're the one who insisted on stopping at the gas station in the first place!" she argued. "Plus, if those boxes had been moved, I could have seen everything much easier. This is your fault, Mitchell."

Mr. Keller rebuffed. "That's not true, and you know it. I would have checked the carrier before leaving, but you didn't. So this is entirely your fault."

Mrs. Keller scoffed. "If it were up to you, the dogs wouldn't have even come with us for the trip. You would've left them behind with Mrs. Stokes, or even worse, the 'doggy hotel' where Zoey died. You just would've made the kids more upset, as usual."

The comment stung Mr. Keller. Their argument was born out of frustration. Both of them had been working non-stop, he at the shop and her with the summer school program. Even with the kids gone at camp, they never had time for themselves. Or the dogs. Not to mention how their finances continued to dwindle in the past few months; money, or the lack thereof, was often another layer of arguments between the two.

The one and only time they had off this summer, they had to pick up their injured son from camp early. And now, their beloved dogs were missing. Mr. Keller sighed, defaulting out of the argument for now. "Let's head back and search before we lose these dogs forever."

Mr. Keller's phone started ringing. He looked at the Caller ID and winced with fear. A gulp let loose in his throat, unsure of what to say. Mrs. Keller didn't have to ask to know who was calling.

"It's the kids."

Chapter 8
Friendly Feline

Sniff, sniff, sniff, sniff.

Summer's nose pondered through the patches of leaves and twigs. With her head low to the ground, the trek forward through the forest came with a *sniff* of excitement and anxiousness. That was until one measly *sniff* into a pollinated cluster of flowers sparked a series of sneezes.

Robin was ahead of Summer by a dozen feet, scouting the mesh of woods and trees. Birds tweeted. Bluejays, cardinals, hummingbirds, and even eagles were everywhere! Squirrels and rabbits dashed by in blurs. Butterflies, like specks, soared silently across the air. A woodpecker working on an oak tree echoed through the landscape. Robin wanted to chase them all, but he also wanted to keep Summer in tow as they entered deeper into unknown territory.

Nature can be a friend, but it also can be an unforgivable foe. This was a lesson they were taught on the RV trip last summer. But the campsites they visited were always surrounded by other people, other families. This was different; the dogs were *alone*.

Uncertain noises spooked them, creating a sense of worry as they wandered about. They had no direct destination in mind. They just wanted to find the Kellers.

They also wanted food; their bellies grew restless from hunger.

Summer lets out a deep *ah-choo!* Her sneeze disturbed a hovering bumblebee. It attempted to soar away, but it was ensnared by a tangly spider web.

The web silently reverberated, warning the neighboring eight-legged harvester of its trapped future snack. It reminded her of the tiny pesky spiders she and Robin would find in the backyard of the Keller house, but this one was much bigger. Spooked by the scene, Summer quickly scurried back to her brother's position.

The grove was green, amber, and lively. But it held evident dangers too. So Robin scouted for a clearing from the woods to understand precisely where they were.

Up ahead, there was a break in the line of trees. A lightning-fast flutter sped by Robin, rocketing towards the clearing. The little creature had wings, and Robin saw its unmistakable white coat. It was a dove.

At the Keller household, there was an antique birdhouse and bird bath in the backyard that was a beacon to the neighborhood flyers. Mr. Keller had built it a long time ago when he and Mrs. Keller first got married; there were still chew marks on the post from Zoey. Doves were the most frequent visitors who would shelter in the birdhouse and bathe in the bath. Mrs. Keller called them birds of good fortune.

Robin's interest was piqued, and he followed the dove into the forest. Again, summer trotted behind him, this time more closely. They wanted to follow the dove diligently without losing it.

Crunching sounds of leaves echoed through the forest. The noise came directly from their left. The puppies' eyes widened as they watched a trio of whitetail deer gallop through the woods. The deer were headed in their direction, so Robin and Summer raced to the opening to avoid the incoming trample.

Near out of breath, the dogs clumsily tripped over one another. Their faces collided right into a mud puddle. Summer released another sneeze. They looked back to spot the sprinting deer, but they had already disappeared into the thickets of the forest.

Thankfully, to their surprise, the open space Robin and Summer stumbled upon had rows of log cabins. It appeared to be a campground. The wooden dwellings offered a beacon of safety for the dogs.

Robin spotted a cottontail rabbit hopping through the yard of the nearest cabin. It noticed the presence of the dogs and, as a result, collided with a clothesline pole. Robin felt tempted to chase the rabbit, but he realized they needed to stay focused. Their surroundings had yet again changed. And this was definitely not the camp that Joey and Annie were staying at.

Then Robin spotted the dove that flew so quickly by him. Petite, plump, and hearty in its chirping, it soared across the greenery, weaving around the string of one-story cabins.

The sky was approaching dusk. A golden hour of sunshine cast along the dormant community. Nightfall was coming fast, and Robin and Summer recognized they needed to move quickly.

They traversed the unfenced yards of the cabins, following the little dove's flight plan. Summer's stomach growled; then Robin's. They were reminded of their appetites growing restless.

One cabin, then two. A makeshift playground, a picnic table. Even a beach volleyball court. So much area to socialize and hang out at –all very new looking too – and yet no people. The only sounds came from the cicadas, crickets, and birds' high-pitched songs and whistles.

The little dove tweeted as it flew its path. The puppies watched the beautiful bird flank left of the last cabin. It continued to fly to a giant wood barn detached from a tiny red house. It was a ranch and sat a few yards away from the row of cabins. Two pickup trucks were parked on the gravel driveway. Lights were turned on in the windows.

The dove directed itself to the barn, soaring through the opened double doors. Robin signaled for the barn, much to Summer's chagrin yet again. She realized their choices were limited. The sunlight kept fading. Reluctantly, she followed her brother into the barn.

Yuck! The stench!

A wave of rancid smells overcame their puppy nostrils. The barn was dimly lit, but it was abundantly clear where the scent derived from. The culprits were stable horses and the aftermath of their meals. Mounds and mounds of manure. It reminded the dogs of when the Kellers took them pumpkin picking last autumn; the pumpkin patch was next to a dingy petting zoo. Joey had a sneezing attack from all the hay.

Half a dozen mares and stallions lined the right side

59

of the barn. Across from the barred stables were tall stacks of hay. The persistent little dove perched itself atop a bale, presenting itself with a perch to look down at the dogs.

Before Robin and Summer could even begin to address their food problem or why they followed the dove in the first place, they sensed another new smell close by. It was not something pungent, but it was a smell of familiarity. Definitely not a horse, but for sure, another animal. They had sensed this type of scent before in their neighborhood when the Kellers would take them for walks.

They heard the subtle sound of a chiming jingle from above. The puppies looked up to the barn beams, as did the dove.

A hiss and a leap!

A giant snow-coated cat descended onto the bale and swiped its claws at the bird with ferocity. The attempt failed. The cat caught nothing but air and some hay. The dove fled; the cat gave up. It was not quick enough.

She turned her attention to the puppies. The cat was a towering monstrosity and way bigger than both dogs. Her icy blue eyes stared quizzically at the two strangers in the barn. Her silver-streaked ears perked skyward. She was clearly annoyed that the dogs witnessed her failure at capturing dinner. With one swift leap, she further descended to the ground floor. This was one cat the dogs were not going to chase.

Robin attempted to sniff her behind, but she raised a clawed paw in protest. He shamefully backed down. She then assessed the dogs and their threat potential, realizing they were no threat. They're simply lost. And hungry.

Her bright purple-threaded collar held a jingle bell and a bronze tag that read *Whisper*.

Despite her massive size, Whisper was a friendly feline – not a foe. She urged the puppies to follow her as she led them past the horses in their stables. Whisper held a pearl of certain wisdom about her. She was older than the puppies and seemed to understand their dire situation.

The closest interaction the dogs have ever had with a cat was when they were first introduced to Grandma Keller's tiny kitten, S'mores. She was named after the treat since her coat was patterned in the same colors as a s'more. Unlike Whisper, she was petite and non-intimidating but laughably ferocious. She would hiss at the dogs whenever they were visiting with Joey and Annie.

The trio exited the back barn door into a meadow of floating pollen. The sun's descent continued; they had a handful of minutes before evening. Fireflies emerged, spotlighting their glowing goldenness throughout the field. Robin and Summer were bemused with fascination. For Whisper, however, it's just another summer night on the homestead.

As they approached the red ranch, they saw a large sign planted in the gravel driveway. It read: *CABIN RENTALS UNDER RENOVATION; OPENING NEXT SEASON*. This explained why the cabins were empty. The farm owners were working on their log cabins for a future grand opening.

Where were the owners of the farm now? Robin and Summer had many questions but were left with no answers.

Whisper kept them close on her trail as she guided them to a small structure on the other side of the ranch. It was a storage shed with a doghouse built into it. A nailed-in wooden sign on the archway of the doghouse read, *Milton*.

The dogs were confused; no other canine was in sight.

Whisper slivered her body through the doghouse connected to the locked storage shed. Robin and Summer did the same. The scents in the doghouse were unmistakable. There's a fuzzy dark blue blanket, a few gnarled chew toys, and an old leash rope that was clearly used for teething. The scent was fresh. A dog was living here.

Robin and Summer also noticed the empty food bowls. Whisper recognized their hunger and trotted further into the shed. She gracefully leaped onto a dusty, elongated shelf. The prize was there! A massive bag of dog kibble! Robin and Summer's eyes widened with envy.

In one swift motion, Whisper knocked the bag over the shelf with her paw. The bag spilled its contents all over the floor. Robin and Summer finally had some chow. The kibble pieces were larger than they were accustomed to, which meant Milton was likely a big dog. They didn't care. It was harder to chew, but they crammed the food pellets down, fulfilling their starvation.

Of course, the dogs were thirsty too, but Whisper was already aware of this. She cautiously slinked her way to another shelf where there was a bucket of rainwater.

Not for long. With another swipe, the pail fumbled over the shelf onto the ground floor. The pups turned their attention to the pail, now gushing out water. Interchangeably, Robin and Summer took turns drinking, quenching their thirsts.

The pail eventually ran dry. There was a mess in the shed, and it became apparent Whisper was the troublemaker in the farmer family. Although she was fond of the small dogs, she did not appear to share the same sentiment or respect for Milton.

Following the replenishment, the sun finally settled. A dark evening sky loomed overhead, and the fireflies multiplied. Whisper motioned the puppies to the blue blanket in the doghouse. She exchanged a friendly, reassuring glance and then slinked away again, this time to the back porch of the ranch house.

Robin and Summer snuggled into the blanket as they watched the friendly feline enter a tiny pet door. They lost view of her, but she reappeared again on the ledge of a bay window. She then nestled into a plush cat bed on the windowsill in a dimly lit living room. It was hard for Summer to see it due to her eyesight, but Robin could easily spot something in the living room. It was a portrait.

The old painting was of a family of four. A little cavalier patterned like Summer was lying on the youngest child's lap. Whisper the cat was in the picture, too. She sat on the other child's lap. Another animal was positioned next to the father, but its face and stature were partially blocked by a standing lamp.

This must be why Whisper was so amicable to them; she was familiar with King Charles Cavaliers. But what happened to the cavalier in the painting, they wondered? The cavalier in the portrait appeared older, so it may have passed away. Maybe Whisper and the cavalier were raised together as pals? Robin wondered about the cavalier's mysterious absence as his sister gently drifted off into sleep. He then rested his eyes, too, thinking about the Keller family and how dearly he missed them.

Chapter 9
Searching and Searching

"Please, please, please tell me you have found them!"

Annie was panicked. Joey was too. But his sense of dread and anxiety was far more severe than his sister's. Either way, they were both upset with their parents. More than upset, they were piping angry.

"Not yet," said Mr. Keller into his cell phone. "Your mother and I have circled the gas station several times."

Francine added, "It's getting late. There's no sunlight left."

"That means it will be harder to find them," said Annie nervously. "Are you using your smartphone flashlight?"

Mr. Keller forgot his phone had that function. However, Mrs. Keller did not. She already had hers turned on and was using it to look around the cedar tree again for any sign of their dogs. It was useless. She knew they wouldn't be there.

The Kellers had been checking the same spots for hours, and nothing had changed. The dogs were missing.

While Mr. Keller was busy on the phone with Annie, Mrs. Keller decided to ask the store clerk if he had seen anything. She was worried Summer and Robin had been stolen, but reviewing surveillance footage revealed they had crossed the dangerous road and entered the endless forest.

"Look, Annie," said Mr. Keller. "We may have to wait until tomorrow morning to get answers."

Before Annie could respond, Mrs. Keller entered the minivan frantically. "They crossed the road about an hour ago. I saw it myself on the surveillance camera. They went that way."

Mrs. Keller pointed towards the forest. Mr. Keller informed the kids.

"The dogs are in a forest across from the gas station, says your mother."

Annie sighed. She understood how spooky it can get in the northern woods. There were barely any lampposts and very few industrial lights. The deeper one traveled into the woods, the darker it became. It would be impossible to continue searching at night.

This worried Annie even more. How will Robin and Summer, *two housebound cavaliers*, survive a night out in the wild? She shuddered at the thought of something happening to them. Her fury for her parents was uncontainable.

But Annie relented and activated her cellphone's speaker function so that Joey could listen in. He had been silent the whole time.

"Joey and I agree. It's better to search in the morning, but we still can't believe you lost the dogs! And after everything that happened with Zoey, what is wrong with the two of you!"

"Blame your mother," quipped Mr. Keller.

The kids could hear their mother yell a rebuttal to their father. Then she took over the phone.

"Can we talk to Joey?" asked Mrs. Keller.

Annie turned to her brother. He shook his head 'no.' Annie was angry, but Joey's expression said it all – he was fuming. Whatever thoughts were running through his head were surely negative.

"No," replied Annie. "He doesn't want to talk to you guys."

A sad silence lingered on the phone call. The Keller parents knew their children were devastated and downright mad. Nothing they could say right now would help the situation. The kids loved the puppies immeasurably. Yet, they felt absolutely let down.

"We're so sorry," said Mrs. Keller, finally breaking the silence. "We will find them. I promise."

Annie wanted to believe it but lost faith in her parents' promises. For months it had been non-stop bickering in the Keller house. Arguments about slacking off in school, screaming matches over Joey's video games, fights about how the Keller parents were overwhelmed with work, and conversations about money running low daily.

Mr. Keller often scratched numbers on a pad. He was doing math that never ended with a positive. He was concerned about how much money he would need to pay for Annie and Joey to attend college. Thus, one of the reasons why he needed them to score high grades – he prayed they'd each receive scholarships to soften the financial blow.

Everything that used to be casual conversation would escalate into full-on arguments. Wilderness World Camp had been an escape, but now they were mucked back into the fray. This time, the well-being of their dogs was involved. A wave of guilt had washed over the twins.

"You need to find them," Annie demanded.

Mrs. Keller responded, "We will, Annie. Tomorrow. I promise."

Mr. Keller chimed in, "We have to hang up, sweetheart. I'm sitting outside the motel, and I fear they'll sell the last room if we don't go in there now."

Annie offered Joey one last chance to take the phone and say something. But again, he shook his head no. Then she hung up.

Annie sat crisscrossed on the end of Joey's cot. He was tucked under his covers, resting his broken wrist on a plush pillow. Joey wanted to cry, but other campers were nearby playing late-night board games and charades. The Keller kids had noticed some friends trying to eavesdrop on the multiple phone calls with Mitchell and Francine.

Kirsten and Emily, friends of Annie, came into the room asking if she wanted to join them in a Connect Four tournament. Annie loved playing Connect Four, but she rejected the offer. This led her friends to sense something was wrong.

Edwin, the camp director – also Kirsten's dad – entered the room with Martha. She was the retired-veteran-turned-camp-nurse whom everyone loved. They wanted to check on the Keller kids.

It was obvious to Annie why they were there. Kirsten and Emily had said something about the dogs being lost. Edwin asked Joey if he and Martha could help. Joey didn't answer, leaving Annie to do all the talking. She explained what had happened to Summer and Robin.

"I can make a few calls to animal control to keep a lookout," Martha said. "My sister Louisa is a veterinarian. If we find the dogs, she can examine them."

"*If* we find the dogs? I prefer *when* we find the dogs," Annie stated with confidence.

Martha agreed. "I stand corrected. *When* we find the dogs."

Boomer, the western terrier, could sense the sadness and angst in Annie and Joey and decided to remain by their side as a cuddly buddy. He laid his furry snowflake head on Annie's lap at the edge of the bed. She patted him graciously.

Joey's pal Austin reentered the cabin. "Do you want to play with us, Joey? We are going to start a game of man-hunt."

Joey, again, remained silent. Annie spoke on his behalf.

"He's going to pass," replied Annie. "We are dealing with family stuff."

Austin accepted her answer and went back out to join the other kids. Annie then turned her attention to Joey. She was annoyed by his silence.

"Joey, you need to speak up, grow up, get up, whatever," demanded Annie. "The silent treatment isn't helping anyone. We need to figure out what we're going to do."

Joey, looking at his injured wrist, finally broke his silence. "It's my fault. If this hadn't happened to me, our dogs would be safe at home."

Annie rolled her eyes. "This isn't the time for a 'poor me' act. It's your fault, it's mom's fault, dad's fault, my fault, heck, even the dogs' fault! Why would they leave the mini-van in the first place? None of it makes sense, but here we are. We need a strategy, Joey."

"There's no strategy, Annie," said Joey.

He looked at Boomer sleeping, thinking about Robin and Summer.

"They're somewhere in the woods. Alone. At night. There is no way they survive. We should just be hoping to find their remains."

Annie wanted to slap her brother for even suggesting they were dead.

"Those dogs are smarter than what you're giving them credit for. They're not gone. They are lost. And it's going to be temporary. Once mom and dad get here, I'm helping in the search for them. If they're in the woods, there's a lot of ground to cover."

Joey knew she was correct.

"You should help us, Joey," she added. "Because we'll need you. Summer and Robin are our family, and they need your help."

Annie left the bed, partially disturbing Boomer's sleep, and went to her cot. Joey rolled to his side, still thinking about the dogs. They had good memories of fetch, the RV trip, and opening gifts at Christmas. But then he thought about the times they were neglected or times that he and Annie could have been better pet owners.

One thing was for sure if they found Robin and

Summer: they would give the dogs the love and attention they deserved. The kids were aware of their recent slacking and knew they were letting their dogs down. That needed to change, pronto.

Joey and Annie hoped that Robin and Summer could pull through and endure one night in the untamed wilderness. Hope was the only thing they could do.

Both twins couldn't sleep that night, knowing Robin and Summer were in the dark. Alone.

~

Crrrrrkkkkk.

Robin heard it. Summer heard it too. Both of their ears raised up. Their tails wagged feverishly. They were on high alert.

The snapping of twigs sounded spooky. The crunchy, breaking noise came from applied pressure that intensified every second. No doubt it was the pressure of a foot. Or a paw. The sound wasn't far away.

Someone, or something, was close by. Very close by.

It was pitch black, and it was late at night. Milton's blanket kept the pups warm, but unexplained noises throughout the night kept them half awake. The croaking of frogs. The chirping of crickets. The scurries of field mice. The wind swayed the tree branches. The noises were everywhere, and they were familiar.

This new sound was different. It was the sound of lurking. The sound of danger.

Robin exited the doghouse to investigate. Summer tentatively followed.

A scent was in the air. Not a dog, nor a cat. Something different. Something wild. A predator of some kind.

A low rumbling growl stirred in Robin and Summer as dashes of incoming rain obstructed their view. It was only a drizzle, but the dogs feared it could get heavier soon.

The pups sensed the predator hiding nearby. Another twig snapped, but this time the sound was even closer.

Then, the distinct sound of an echoing bellow rang out. A *hooting sound*. The pups turned their attention to the treetops. They saw a shadowy figure emerging with unblinking yellow eyes that were fixated on Robin and Summer.

A series of hoots followed, but not in their direction. Instead, a great-horned owl hooted toward the thick dark bushes. The giant owl was directing its attention at the lurking predator.

The owl's hooting foiled the predator's plan, revealing the secret spot. A wiggle movement rattled the bush. A four-legged animal dashed out from the hiding spot, away from the dogs and the owl, retreating deep into the woods.

It ran so fast that it was too difficult to determine its species. But then, a flash of lightning illuminated the rainy forest, unveiling a glance at the predator from behind. It had a crimson-colored tail.

The rain turned into a downpour. Robin and Summer retreated back to the doghouse. They snuggled even closer together. Fear and adrenaline were surging through their small bodies.

They both looked at the birch where the male owl sat like a gargoyle. He was unfazed by the rainfall. His glowy gold eyes stared, again, directly at the dogs. But not as a predator, as a protector.

Robin was comfortable with the owl's presence; he felt a sense of security because Joey used to read no less than five comic books a night. He would read them aloud to Robin. One of his comics had a superhero who would dress thematically after an owl. The story claimed the owl hero was a guardian to all he protected and that the owls were full of wisdom and guidance.

This owl remained perched on his leafy branch. The dogs tried to maintain a staring contest. The owl refused to blink and remained impressively still.

Soon, Summer tired out and fell asleep. Robin tried to hold his gaze, but he, too, succumbed to tiredness. Within minutes the puppies were sleeping again, and the owl remained in his position.

Meanwhile, deep in the woods, a devilish predator remained close by. He awaited an opportunity to strike his prey, Summer and Robin.

Chapter 10
The Reality of the Nightmare

A blend of violet and orange colored the morning sky. Storm clouds continued to recede. The aftermath of an overnight rainstorm glistened across the damp meadow. Finally, the peaking rays of the rising sun stirred Robin and Summer awake. They yawned and stretched their little bodies. Both dogs noticed the owl was absent from his perch.

Before they could relieve themselves in the grassy knolls, they saw a creature running through the mist. It was Whisper the cat. She appeared to be alarmed. Her whiskered face and terrified eyes said it all – the dogs needed to *go*. And *fast*. Her attention turned to the porch door.

But their bladders were full, so they quickly attempted to relieve themselves. That's when they saw what Whisper tried warning about. It was Milton. A large, juvenile German Shepherd. Feelings of panic and terror overtook Robin and Summer.

The enormous German Shepherd bolted through the back door of the porch. He was barking loudly as he ran towards the yard. He stopped in his tracks for a moment to sniff the air and detected a foreign scent he didn't like. His demeanor turned vicious.

Like Robin, Milton's furry coat was an arrangement of midnight black and bronze, with speckles of white near his face. But unlike Robin and his sister, Milton was a monster. He outweighed them by eighty pounds easily.

The sight of Milton emitted a *hiss* from Whisper. It became more evident why she was not a fan of her fellow house pet. The giant dog was a powerhouse of aggression and immaturity.

Milton's attention shifted to the doghouse. Robin and Summer stood frozen in place. They had been spotted.

"What is it, Milton?" asked an older gentleman from the porch screen door.

The old man was wearing a maintenance jumpsuit. He had thick eyeglasses and was holding a tool bag. He had not seen Robin and Summer.

Milton released a thunderous, deafening series of barks that echoed in the early morning air, then charged toward the puppies.

Everything happened so fast. Milton stampeded through the meadow like a cheetah. With no other way of helping the pups, Whisper retreated to the shed. Robin and Summer were on their own.

The pups ran. They ran with all their might, but they ran in circles. They had no clue as to where they should go. Where was the safest direction?

Summer took charge. She barked at Robin, indicating she wanted her brother to follow her lead. She headed toward a thicket of trees in the bordering forest, and Robin followed behind. Milton's running was four times the speed of the puppies. The massive canine closed in. His barks grew louder and more hostile, capturing the attention of the older gentleman on the porch.

"What in the heck is going on out there?" yelled the old man.

In perilous distress, Robin and Summer sprinted headfirst towards the area where the crimson-tailed predator was spotted the night before. The dogs knew the risks of the predator still lurking about, but Milton was beyond intimidating. So they took the chance.

Summer and Robin dashed into the shrubbery filled with sharp vines and prickly leaves. They cut their paws, ears, and tails on thorny branches. But the pain did not stop the chase. Milton was a few yards away.

Robin and Summer wiggled their way out of the shrubbery. Robin was panicked. So much so that he tumbled down a ditch after escaping the shrubs. Summer avoided the fall but tripped in a mid-air jump over an unrooted oak trunk.

Milton, with unstoppable force, walloped into the shrubbery – not minding the pain of the thorns. His head and torso breached the thicket, and he turned his attention to Robin. He was still dazed from his fall into the ditch and quickly realized he lacked an escape.

Milton let out a distraught yelp as he lunged forward into the ditch, but his body failed to move. Snared between his neck and collar was a string of vine, firmly wrapped in place. Furiously, he tried to wiggle his neck loose, but the vine was too thick and intertwined. He was utterly trapped.

Both Robin and Summer acted fast. Summer snatched a long branch and tried to lower it to Robin. His jowls latched on, and Summer used her strength to guide Robin out of the deep ditch. Meanwhile, Milton was making progress on chewing off the vine. The old man was gaining closer to their position too. However, he was now clutching a double-barreled shotgun instead of a tool bag.

Without hesitation or pause, the cavaliers sprinted deeper into the forest. Far away from the farm. Far away from Milton. Far away from danger. Or so they hoped.

~

At Wilderness World Camp, Joey continued to feel anxious about the missing dogs. His anxiety carried over into his sleep. His favorite dreams were now turning into nightmares.

All of a sudden, Joey is back in his hometown. With Annie, Robin and Summer. They are running around the neighborhood park. He and Annie are teasing the dogs by holding the squeaky toys – a duck and a snake. Naturally, the dogs chase after them.

Annie plays tug of war with Summer; her puppy strength is impressive. She clenches the fake snake and will not let go. Annie is laughing.

Robin is fast in his pursuit of the duck. He loves the duck toy. Joey is relentless, testing Robin's endurance. He swipes the duck left and right in the air; Robin leaps after it each time. Joey lobs the toy duck far down the field in one long, far toss. Maybe too far. It soars out of view.

Robin chases after it. Summer too. They keep running, fading out of view. Now, they are long gone.

"Joey, what did you do?" asks Annie.

Panic sets in. They should have returned by now. Where are the dogs?

Joey calls out their names. "Robin! Summer!"

"They're gone."

"Where did they go?!"

Joey hears Annie's words being repeated over and over again... "Joey, what did you do? Joey, what did you do? Joey, what did you do?"

Joey sprung up from his pillow. He was awake now; he took a gasp. His nightmare felt so very real and permanent. He could feel the sweat stains on his arm cast and bed sheets.

Annie was standing by the edge of his bed. Next to her was Edwin. Boomer, too.

"Joey, you had another dream. Let's go; get yourself together. Mom and dad are almost here," said Annie.

"You okay, champ?" asked Edwin.

Boomer jumped on the bed and began licking the sweat off Joey's cheeks.

"I'm fine," replied Joey in a groggy tone. "Give me a few minutes to get dressed."

When he turned six years old, Joey developed a condition where he was prone to night terrors. They would usually get triggered during times of stress, anxiousness, or even sadness. The Keller parents took him to a doctor after a week of non-stop nightmares, but the doctor claimed it was something Joey would grow out of in time. Some nights, Annie would sleep in the same room as her brother to help quell the nightmares. She was eventually replaced by Robin, who became Joey's beacon of emotional support whenever a nightmare hit.

But now, Joey's night terrors were about the dogs he loved. This was something new. Before the dogs were lost, the nightmares usually involved mythical monsters under the bed or evil ghosts roaming the halls. Things that simply didn't exist were Joey's enemies; things that couldn't hurt him in real life were Joey's concerns. But this morning, things were much different. The nightmare he woke up to was a presentation of his current reality. Summer and Robin were missing.

A sense of dread washed over Joey as he dressed for the day. He looked at his watch. Almost an entire twenty-four hours had passed since the dogs' disappearance. The more time wasted, the lesser the chance of finding Summer and Robin alive. He calculated the odds. Little hope remained for a positive turnout. Joey's thoughts ran wild. He imagined every worst-case scenario as he put on his socks.

A tear formed in Joey's eye as he laced his sneakers. And then the door opened; it was Annie. He didn't want her to see him cry. Joey rubbed the top of his own head, trying to drown out the dark thoughts. He turned to Annie with a fake smile, "I'm ready to go."

The Keller kids were sitting anxiously on the old bench at the end of the long dirt road leading to the main camp entrance. They sprung to their feet when seeing their parents make the turn onto the road. The minivan traveled at high speed, causing the dirt to kick up and form dust clouds. Mitchell and Francine knew time wasn't on their side.

Mr. Keller slowed down considerably as he approached the camp entry sign. He could see the kids. They were accompanied by Edwin, Boomer, and camp nurse Martha. He parked the minivan and took a deep breath. Then, he turned to his wife and said, "This isn't going to be fun."

Grim faces were stuck on Mrs. and Mr. Keller. They had spent the early morning showing photographs of the dogs to local residents, but the effort was useless. Nobody had seen Summer and Robin. And now they had to face their children.

Before the Keller parents exited the minivan, both kids rushed to hug them. Joey hugged their mom; Annie hugged their dad. It was not the reaction Mitch and Fran expected after losing Robin and Summer.

"We're so sorry," said Mrs. Keller as tears rose.

Mr. Keller put his hands on Annie's cheeks and looked her straight in the eye. Mitchell wasn't the warmest of men, but his heart was speaking loudly at this moment. "Your mom and I love those dogs as much as you do, and we love the two of you more than anything in the world," added Mr. Keller.

Tears streamed down Joey and Annie's faces. As upset and angry as they were, they couldn't hold back the emotions flooding them. They hadn't seen their parents in weeks. But the affectionate hugs did not last long.

Joey retracted from his mother, his face distraught. "You're always on us about being responsible when it comes to Robin and Summer. And yet you're the one who ends up being irresponsible. How could you leave them? How can you leave the parking lot without ensuring they were okay?"

Mrs. Keller sighed. "Joey, I screwed up. There was so much going on in the car, and we rushed to get up here to help take care of your wrist. It was a mistake, and I'll always regret it."

"It wasn't a mistake. You were careless," claimed Joey.

"Go easy on your mother," demanded Mr. Keller.

Joey turned to his father, staring at him with anger and accusation. "What's your excuse, dad? You should have checked on them. Maybe you should be as attentive to the dogs as you are to me playing video games."

"Don't you disrespect me, Joseph Keller," countered Mr. Keller in a stern voice.

He continued, "I understand you're upset; everyone is upset. But I'm your father, and she's your mother. We're not perfect and made a mistake, but you will not talk to us in that tone of voice. You will not disrespect your parents no matter how upset you are."

Sensing they should give the family some room, Edwin and Martha took Boomer for a stroll on the other side of the road.

Knowing her father was turning his energy in a direction that would not help Summer and Robin, Annie took a smoother approach.

"Dad, Joey has been having nightmares about the dogs. He doesn't mean to be disrespectful. I think he's trying to say that if the situation was reversed, we would be punished and scolded to no end."

"Come on, Annie, you're exaggerating," replied Mrs. Keller.

"No, mom, I am not. Joey and I spoke about it a lot during these past few weeks. Truthfully, we feel like the two of you are always expecting perfection from us!"

"That's not true," said Mrs. Keller. "We pushed a little harder this year because we saw you slipping. We want you to strive to be your best, and we know it's not easy when there are so many distractions in our lives. That's why we sent you to camp. And I know it's my fault, but the dogs will be fine. We need to think positive thoughts."

His mother's calming message didn't do the trick. Joey stood defiant with his arms folded. He looked to his sister for guidance, but Annie said nothing. Instead, she bowed her head and swirled the dirt on the ground with her right foot.

Mr. Keller chimed in. "You need to grow up now! And I mean both of you. The situation is bad. We know the dogs are out there in the woods, and we are all determined to find them. But make no mistake. The dogs will never be found if we don't work as a team. So, as your team leader, I am telling you that it starts with the Kellers sticking together as a family. We need to lift each other up versus tearing each other down. Does this make sense?"

Annie responded, "Yes, dad."

Francine nodded her head in agreement.

Joey unlocked his arms. He wiped the tears from his face.

"How about you, Joey?" asked Mr. Keller.

His son nodded. "Let's get going. I'm ready if you are."

Mr. Keller waved over Edwin and Martha.

"Edwin, I think we should start searching the different sections of woods together, but in groups."

Edwin responded, "Absolutely. You've got our commitment that we'll keep looking until we find Robin and Summer."

"We appreciate that," said Mr. Keller.

"But I can't lie to you, Mitchell. There are lots of elements to overcome in those woods," added Edwin. "Bear, snakes, mountain lions, fox. I want you to realize that the deeper we go, the more dangerous it becomes."

Joey exclaimed, "There's no way the dogs will survive."

The Kellers stood silent, pondering the dogs' chances of surviving those woods. It would take a miracle, though no one wanted to admit that. But before anyone could say anything, they were interrupted with surprising news.

Martha had received a call on her cell phone. The festive ringtone prompted Boomer to bark. She hushed Boomer to be quiet and answered the phone. The Kellers could see Martha's face brighten with a wide grin as she listened to the voice on the other end.

"It's animal rescue," said Martha. "They just received news about Robin and Summer!"

Chapter 11
The Roaring River

Robin and Summer panted with tongues hung low. They were dehydrated, tired, and hurt. They ran until their paws felt scratched and inflamed. They were left with no choice.

Robin and Summer's encounter with Milton the German Shepherd left them exhausted and, yet again, lost in the woods. The early morning shifted towards a sunny afternoon. They did not stop moving, no matter how worn out they were.

Eventually, Summer demanded a pause in their journey. They were clear from the immediate danger of Milton, and she felt it was time to get their bearings. Robin relented, realizing they needed to gain an awareness of their current surroundings.

Wherever they were, it was definitely far from any human life. The woods appeared endless in its lush green forestry. The tree-top coverage was immense, too, with only a distant mountain in view. No clearings were visible. They were in the heart of the great outdoors. They would have to rely on specific scents, sounds, and instincts to find a sense of direction.

On the RV trip last summer, the Kellers constantly mentioned that if anyone ever got lost in the hiking trails, they should always search for higher ground. It would make rescuers easier to spot you from the air, but the higher elevation grants you the ability to better scout where you are.

Mr. Keller mentioned a story about how his brother was lost on a deep trail in the Alaskan wilderness. He was stranded for three days, but it could have been longer had he not scaled up an incline onto the cliffside of a mountain. Rescue helicopters were able to quickly spot him. They said that had he remained in the thrush of the forest, he would never have been found.

The dogs looked at the mountain. It was positioned in the direction of the north. Instinct told them the mountain would be a starting point.

Robin and Summer stayed low to the ground, embracing their genetic instincts. Before heading north, the first priority was water.

Water had the potential to lead them on a path to civilization, but more importantly, it would quench their growing thirst. If they did not drink soon, they would only move slower, physically and mentally, as the day continued.

Robin sniffed aggressively eastward while Summer veered to the west. Robin's search fell short. All he could hear were birds chirping, including the nearby hooting of a roaming owl. Before he could dwell on its whereabouts, he heard Summer bark.

She sensed a peculiar scent. Wandering further into a thicket of lilac flowers, the smell grew more intense as she scurried closer.

A forceful ejection of mist sprayed from within the flower bush, enveloping Summer. Robin ran to his sister and was also tagged with a smaller dose of the spray. The scent was repugnant, vomit-inducing, and eye-watering.

The cavaliers spotted the black-and-white striped culprit on the opposite end of the bush. A nefarious, nifty skunk. It looked frightened.

The skunk realized his mistake in the sudden stink attack; the pups did not present a threat. Robin and Summer retreated from the stinky vermin, heading northbound. Robin maintained a not-so-subtle distance from Summer and her coated skunk stench. The smell was truly unbearable. Still, they trekked on and wandered into an area of fallen logs.

Robin picked up another scent. Not the skunk, nor a cat, nor a squirrel. And not the mysterious owl, either. It was a different scent, almost piney in smell. He heard a light scratching sound as if two pieces of sandpaper were rubbing together. It reminded him of Mr. Keller sanding in his work-shop. Robin sniffed aggressively, with his snout leading him into a hollow log.

Thoink! A big, pointy mistake. Robin yelped in pain as he backed away. Exiting the log was a salt-and-peppered porcupine. One of her quills nicked Robin's nose. Luckily, it was only a scratch. But the angry porcupine lurked in Robin's direction. It was annoyed at the dog's intrusion into her home.

Robin ran back to Summer, who saw the spiky rodent and wanted no interaction. They continued traversing through the fallen logs, hoping to avoid other creatures that could harm them.

Summer took the lead as Robin pawed at the scratch on his snout. No blood was drawn, but the quill definitely irritated his skin. Every time he sniffed, it felt like someone was flicking his nostrils.

A rushing sound could be heard. They both remained cautious following the skunk and porcupine encounters, but the dogs recognized the sound was most certainly water. And the sound grew louder as they trekked north. Summer, unlike Robin at the moment, could sniff out the source. She could smell the drifting mist of what she guessed was a stream.

As they approached the water, the dogs realized it was not a stream. Instead, it was a roaring river! Summer and Robin sprinted ahead as the large swath of turquoise water came into view. The winding river ran from west to east. Every few seconds, pink-bellied salmon hurled out of the water and then crashed back in with gusto. The river was also peppered with floating logs and wood debris.

Robin and Summer rushed to the water's edge and began gulping ferociously. The cool, brisk water felt relieving on Robin's scratched nose. Summer dunked her head in with the hope of ridding of the skunk smell. She then dipped her whole body into a still pool of river water; Robin playfully joined her. The water's coldness was relieving after trekking in the hot sun.

They needed to further address their whereabouts. Where did this river lead to? Was it their best chance to find civilization again? Or even the Keller family? Or should they continue traveling to the mountain?

Instinct told them that following the river's flow might be better. Last year when the Kellers brought the dogs on the RV trip, they had stopped at an old, rustic mill town.

At the heart of the town was a man-made dam controlling the oncoming flow of river water. Perhaps the dogs could follow the river's direction eastward, hoping to locate a similar dam.

The dogs' plotting was interrupted by the arrival of a new scent. A familiar scent. A recent one, too. Robin and Summer quit splashing in the water pool and waddled to shore. They froze dead in their tracks, recognizing the origin of the scent. A predatory scent.

It was a fox. A large, skulking male red fox. He stood menacingly a few yards away. His fur had swashes of firestorm orange and red. Its ears were bolted upright, and its thick tail swooshed with a sinister nature. However, the most frightening aspect of the fox was his eyes. They glowed an insidious, dark yellow, centered by shadowy pupils. The fox's eyes gazed directly at his newfound prey.

This was the spying predator from last night when the owl saved Robin and Summer. The fox had intended to eat the dogs. They would have been his late-night dinner. Now, he wanted them for an afternoon feast.

The dogs had never encountered a fox before but were told stories by Joey and Annie about them lurking in the wild. They were always cautioned to stay away from foxes. And now, they were face-to-face with one. A big one.

The fox took an eerie step forward. The pups remained frozen in place. Based on his build, the fox was at least three times the size of Robin and Summer. The dogs had the two-on-one advantage, but the fox had the predatory strength. It was a match-up destined for failure for Summer and Robin.

They had no choice except one. Run!

And they did. With a quick pivot, both dogs sprinted along the river's shoreline as fast as they could. The fearless fox leaped into the chase. He tailed the dogs at first but continued to gain on them.

All three animals attempted to traverse and dodge tree debris along the river bank. Looping through logs, squirming through branches. In less than a minute, the fox was only a few feet behind Summer and Robin. He attempted to take a biting snap at Summer but just missed her tail and tumbled forward. This gave the pups a few more seconds to further the distance.

Quickly, without much thought, they resorted to one last hope. They hopped straightaway into the roaring river, but Robin's collar caught onto a thick branch from a fallen trunk. As the fox leaped for another swipe, he wiggled his neck and head loose from the collar. In the nick of time, Robin freed himself and tumbled into the water next to Summer. The fox stayed put on the log, examining the fate of the dogs.

The water was too deep to stand. Swimming frantically, Summer climbed onto a floating log. She nudged and helped Robin up as well. It was a sturdy log with enough room for the two to cling onto for dear life.

As for the fox, he patrolled the shoreline, following after the dogs. He refused to jump into the water. Instead, he darted up ahead, searching for stationary logs that he could climb. Doing so would bring him closer to his prey.

Fearfully, the dogs watched as the fox found a dis-lodged pine tree. It was hanging overhead, not too far up the river. With no time to waste, he scaled the fallen tree and waited for the dogs to float closer. Robin and Summer braced for his clawed swipes.

Swish, swish! The claws narrowly miss Summer, then Robin. The dogs retreated from the swipes, trying not to stumble into the water. Another *swish!* The fox's swipe nabbed Summer's ear. Robin tried to swipe back but slid into the water. He clung dearly to the soaked wood and pulled himself back onto the log with all his might.

The fox geared up for another swipe but stopped. The log surpassed the fallen tree, and the dogs floated out of range. However, their small victory was again interrupted as they looked ahead to where the river ended. The situation ahead looked impossible to survive.

Chapter 12
The Danger of Nature

"Milton found them scurrying into the bushes over there."

Felix, a farmer and the owner of the upcoming North Valley Cabins Club, pointed toward where his backyard ended before becoming the forest. On the border of the grounds sat his German Shepherd's doghouse.

He was showing the Keller family where Milton had spotted their cavaliers.

"I believe they got into the barn and doghouse, too," said Felix. "There was a mess of kibble and spilled water, and they were sleeping on Milton's blanket. Milton likes to hang out there during the day, but at night he stays inside with my wife and me."

Felix's wife, Verona, brought a tray of lemonade and iced tea to the porch for the Keller family. The couple's house cat, Whisper, trailed behind and cozied between Joey and Annie's legs.

Both Felix and Verona were older, somewhere in their late sixties. Felix sported his dirty maintenance jumpsuit and thick-framed glasses, and his balding head was covered with a trucker's hat. Verona wore a floral dress and had her curly hair tied into a bun. She spoke with a hint of an Italian accent.

"We called animal rescue immediately after they were spotted," said Verona. "They mentioned they were called in about a lost pair of cavaliers. And if they went missing at the gas station, that's not too far from our campgrounds."

"Edwin and Martha are good friends of ours," added Felix. "Our two daughters went to Wilderness World Camp years ago when it was run by Edwin's father; now they are employed at Yellowstone National Park as rangers. They grow up so fast, but we're proud of them."

The Kellers were sitting on bright red Adirondack chairs on the porch. Mr. Keller took a gulp of lemonade, racking his brain with this newfound information given to them by Felix and Verona. There was an urgency to their situation, but the Kellers did not want to be rude guests. As lovely as the lemonade and iced tea presentation was, the Keller family wanted to get moving. But Mr. Keller wanted to make sure these people indeed spotted their dogs.

"We're thankful we were able to get in touch, and we thank you for your hospitality, but time is of the essence here," said Mr. Keller. "You're positive you saw these two cavalier dogs?"

Mr. Keller held up pictures of the dogs on his phone. Verona nodded her head with a chuckle. "Felix's eyesight might be giving out, but we once had a cavalier. Hoagie was named after the first sandwich we had when our family adopted him. He passed away, but he looked almost exactly like one of the pups he saw this morning."

She pointed to their family portrait in the living room. Both Joey and Annie were standing by the window. Annie's eyes lit up.

"He looks just like Summer," exclaimed Annie. She could see some resemblance to Zoey too. "So you really did see them! Where did they go?"

Felix shrugged, fixing his spectacles. "We don't venture too often into those woods; it's too dangerous and wild out there. Also, ever since our town went through some budget cuts, fewer people have gone on hikes because our state troop force has been reduced. So if you get lost out there now, you will be out there on your own."

Annie and Joey's eyes widened with fear, but before they could respond, they heard loud barking. It was Milton, the German Shepherd. He was treading through the meadow, still scouting for the mystery dogs he had encountered earlier. Felix hailed him over. At first, he did not listen. Milton still had some immaturity and behavioral issues with training. But then Felix whistled louder this time, and Milton came sprinting to the porch, tongue wagging and waiting for his next command.

"We can try searching back there if you'd like, even though it is quite dangerous," said Felix. "Milton is great with scouting. He might be able to track them down out there. But I will be bringing some protection too."

Felix entered his house, fiddled with a lockbox next to the door, and brought out a double-barreled shotgun. He started loading the gun with ammunition, keeping the safety trigger locked.

"Is that needed for this kind of search?" asked Mrs. Keller, wondering why he would need a shotgun to find two small dogs.

"Absolutely, it's needed," confirmed Felix. "I don't mean to spook you folks, but out here in these woods, you must stay armed and alert for the wild animals. It's predators galore. In fact, a few years ago, a fox the size of a wolf went after Hoagie. I had to ring out a shot from the gun to scare it off."

The family recalled Edwin's warning about all the wild animals lurking in the woods. As off-putting as the shotgun's presence was, they were glad Felix was bringing it.

Felix attempted to change his tone for the sake of the kids. "Your dogs are probably fine. The shotgun is just for precaution. Same with Milton."

Much to her annoyance, the German Shepherd scooted past Whisper and went to Felix for ear scratches. The big dog was ready to search and rescue the pups he chased away this morning.

"I'll go with Felix and Milton," volunteered Mr. Keller. "You three should stay here with Verona if Summer and Robin come running this way."

Annie and Joey shook their heads simultaneously in disagreement. There was no chance they wouldn't be involved in the search.

"Those dogs are our best friends, dad," said Joey. "Broken wrist or not, I'm coming."

"Me too," added Annie.

Mr. Keller did not push back. Instead, he and the two kids headed for the woods along with Felix and Milton. Mrs. Keller, Verona, and Whisper waited on the porch.

Mrs. Keller had her phone ready in case she were to

get a call about the dogs being found. She also asked Verona if she could use her printer to create more *lost dog* signs with photos of Robin and Summer.

The search party was equipped with flashlights as dusk approached. Felix taped his flashlight to his shotgun. Mrs. Keller and Verona watched as Felix, Mr. Keller, Annie, Joey, and Milton entered the forest.

Mrs. Keller nervously sipped on her warming iced tea. "Thank you for helping us. I really hope we find them."

Verona patted Mrs. Keller's hand. "I remember how much we loved Hoagie. He was so special to us, as Robin and Summer are to you all. It's our pleasure to help."

~

As the floating log approached the waterfall, the whistling wind hovering over the river grew stronger, and so did the river itself. Robin and Summer watched in wide-eyed terror as more debris descended the river's drop-off. It was a steep waterfall, at least thirty feet in its height.

Robin broke from his trance. He glanced over his shoulder, searching for the fox. But the fox had abandoned his post on the fallen overhang tree and was nowhere to be found. It didn't matter. The dogs were faced with an entirely new, more pressing threat.

They had a handful of minutes before reaching the river's end. Toppling over the edge was not an option; they would never make it. Typically, the bottom of waterfalls is laden with stone and rock. Their little dog bodies would be crushed. And to retreat to the southern shoreline came the possibility of encountering the devious fox. Summer and Robin were unwilling to take a chance with him either.

The only solution was to swim to the northern shoreline. However, swimming was not going to be easy. The river's momentum significantly gained as they inched closer to the waterfall. Robin and Summer would have to swim like never before. Their lives depended on it.

Robin jumped in first, followed by Summer. Their small legs paddled as fast as they could against the rushing tide. They continued to drift toward the river's drop-off as the tide's power increased with waves – they were facing wild water topped with white caps. But they persisted in their swim, gaining closer to the shoreline.

Both dogs were nearly bonked in the struggle with a floating tree trunk. They ducked under the blue water, wading through a school of salmon. The silvery pink fish swam in figure-eight formations around the dogs, puzzled by their presence in the river.

They were yards away from the shoreline; they still had quite a distance to swim. The chances of making it grew slimmer by the second.

Summer spotted the outstretched, broken tree branch on the northern shoreline. A few feet from the waterfall, it went about halfway into the water. She barked and began swimming diagonally in its direction; Robin treaded behind her.

They could hear the whomping sound of water crashing into a large body of rocks. The danger lurking below was undeniable.

The dogs were fatigued from the swim; maintaining their heads above the uneven surface grew near impossible. In addition, both dogs had swallowed lots of water in this river plunge, making them feel more sluggish.

The sounds grew deafening as the waterfall drew closer. They had a hairline chance of reaching the protruding branch, so they paddled harder. They extended their necks to clutch the branch but wading through the frenzy of salmon made matters even more daunting.

Summer's attention was focused on what was in front of her; she could see the drop off more visibly. It was a vacuum of doom leading to a watery grave. She could also see an eerie flock of vultures circling above the waterfall, anticipating the dogs to be their next meal.

But she then saw the branch – it was at arm's length. She propelled forward, using the remaining energy in her muscles. She climbed onto the thick branch, easing herself into a steady, safe position.

However, more panic set in; there was no sign of Robin.

Summer started barking. She did not care if it alerted the fox. Her brother was missing. There was no way she could continue on without her beloved companion.

She prepared to jump back into the water when she heard a rustling. Behind her, she saw Robin. He was on the outer head of the giant branch, breaching towards the waterfall. His jaws clamped fiercely on a stringy twig, slowly ripping from the branch.

Robin was about three feet from the waterfall; the ferocious current was attempting to overtake his little body and hurl him over. His only means of preventing the fall was clenching tightly to a twig extending from the branch.

Snap! The twig broke slightly, nearly catapulting Robin forward into the waterfall. Summer acted without hesitation. She scurried to the outer edge of the branch as the vultures swooped in closer, readying for a feast.

With a swift motion, Summer bit into the opposite side of the thick twig, snapping it from the branch. But she held the twig firmly in her jaws while Robin held on to his side for dear life. Then, using all her might, Summer pulled and pulled. She was determined to pull Robin closer to the log.

The roaring water presented a considerable challenge, but now the vultures circled closer. The ugly birds were a terrible distraction, but Summer persisted. She knew she had to save him. It was far more complicated than pulling Robin out of the ditch earlier this morning. Still, the current circumstances equated to life or death.

The dogs stared into each other's eyes. Summer's look was that of unbridled love and determination. Robin's look was of massive fear and great desperation. Both knew this was it. They had one chance, or it was goodbye forever.

Summer anchored her paws into the branch and reinforced her teeth into the twig. She used every fiber in her being to pull Robin from death. Robin let out a small cry of worry. Summer growled as her adrenaline took over. She would need to leverage her anger to find the additional strength required to save her brother.

Summer pulled her head back to the left to lift Robin to the branch. But it didn't work; the twig slipped slightly from Robin's grasp. Summer knew she was losing him. Her instinct said to try one more time; again, she would pull left. Robin clenched the twig even harder, and then with one colossal pull, Summer nudged him higher. Robin used his right paw to grab the branch. Immediately, Summer pulled again. Robin could now catch the branch with his left paw. Summer pulled one last time using all of her might. This lifted Robin a few inches higher but, at the same time, forced the twig from his mouth. But Robin was spry. He got his two hind legs onto the branch. He was saved with only a second to spare.

Exasperated, both dogs sat on the branch. The vultures dispersed with disappointment. But, despite their tiredness, Summer and Robin did not want to take any chances. So the dogs carefully crawled nice and slowly across the big branch until they reached the northern shoreline.

They were drenched and cold. Both dogs shook their coats to dry off. The sun helped by partially drying them, but the sky grew with incoming clouds. The dogs were still damp and were even more laggard now.

Robin and Summer strolled away from the river's shore and collapsed in a weed patch. A few mosquitoes attempted to bother them, but their exhaustion outweighed the care to swat the bugs away. They needed a brief break before returning to the nightmare of escaping the never-ending forest. They did not want to think about the approaching evening, the fox, or how they would be forced to spend another night lost in the wild.

They simply wanted to rest. But they could not. The sound of crackling thunder shook the sky. More rain would be coming soon. Reluctantly, the dogs chugged forward into the woodlands hoping to find another place for shelter.

Unsuspecting to the dogs, a half-mile up the river, the fire-colored predator, was looking for an opening to cross the river and reach the other side. He was persistent; he would not stop until he finished the hunt.

Chapter 13
Evidence

Milton the German Shepherd sniffed and scouted without pause. Eventually, his snout picked up a putrid scent, watering his eyes. It was something terribly foul.

"Milton, come back, boy," ushered Felix. "There's a skunk over there. I'd stay back too, Kellers, unless you want to smell like hot garbage for hours."

The search party consisting of Mr. Keller, Joey, Annie, Felix, and his loyal canine Milton had been in the forest for over an hour. Both the kids and Mr. Keller called out for Robin and Summer interchangeably. The only returning sounds were the caws and hymns of nearby birds.

Milton scoured every crevice and hiding spot in the areas they searched. He had managed to cover more ground than the humans, but his search had turned up nothing except for the horribly smelling skunk.

"It worries me if they got this far," Joey said, nervously plucking at his wrist cast.

The forest had him spooked, knowing what could be creeping within it. He could only imagine what Robin and Summer must be feeling.

"I bet the dogs are somewhere near this area," said Felix. "We're only a stone's throw away from the river that cuts through the forest. Are your dogs swimmers?"

Both Keller kids shook their heads *no*.

Felix nodded with grimness.

Joey and Annie looked at each other with worry. They didn't have a pool at home, so they never trained the dogs properly to swim. A few times on the RV trip, they brought the dogs into a lake. But those were hardly training sessions. Most of the time, Robin and Summer kept to shallow parts where they could stand. A fierce river was a whole different ballpark.

"Where does the river lead to?" asked Mr. Keller with an edgy look.

"The river falls into a nearby lake that is deep and five miles long, and then it turns back into a river."

"When you say it falls into the lake, do you mean a waterfall?" asked Annie.

"Yes. It's a thirty-foot drop."

The kids and Mr. Keller felt more doom settle on their minds. Would the dogs have been silly enough to swim in a river that leads into a waterfall?

"We need to get to the river," said Joey sternly.

Joey took off running, with Annie and Milton following behind him.

"Kids, you know I can't run like that anymore!" shouted Mr. Keller after them.

But Mitch's remarks only echoed in the forest; the kids kept going, leaving him and Felix behind.

Felix said, "Don't worry, Mitch, we'll catch up to them."

Felix eyed the falling sun. There would be twenty minutes until nightfall. Clouds started rolling in. "Mitchell, what will you tell the kids if we have to call off the search?"

"Call off the search? Why would we do that?" asked Mitch.

"I'll be honest; the second night in the wild will be even harder for two small dogs to survive," said Felix.

Mr. Keller sighed. "Whatever I tell the kids is going to break their hearts. It will be as if we lost someone in our family, and to make matters worse, it comes with the burden of knowing that *we* failed them. And I don't know how we will recover considering this past year – it has been so hard on all of us."

Mr. Keller caught himself spilling his emotions a little too much, but Felix wasn't bothered by the confessions. He, too, was a dad, and he understood the pressure that was mounting on Mr. Keller.

Felix rested his shotgun and rested his hand on his new friend's shoulder. "The importance of family can't be emphasized enough, Mitch. There will always be loss; what matters is how you heal together as a family. May I share something personal with you?"

Mr. Keller nodded, not expecting Felix to become the one opening up. His face portrayed a sense of grief.

Felix picked up his gun and started walking and talking.

"When I was a boy, I had a tight family," Felix reminisced. "That was until my only brother, Burke, became ill very young. Before we could blink our eyes or even find a good doctor, he was gone."

"My condolences," said Mitchell.

Felix continued. "It caught us all by surprise. And we never recovered because we never healed together. All we did was fight and pass the blame for Burke's death, yet it was no one's fault. Even so, my father left my mother and me. And mom went into a deep depression. Our family of four just vanished in a matter of months. It wasn't until I met Verona, and we created our own family, that I realized the value in those bonds."

Mitchell replied, "I'm sorry that happened to you."

"So many people take family for granted," continued Felix. "Without family, life just isn't the same. I can tell a man like yourself understands this sort of thing, so I have no doubt you'll get matters corrected. You must focus on keeping the Keller bond strong, whether you find the dogs or not."

Mr. Keller appreciated Felix's faith in his abilities as a father and husband. But deep inside, Mitch felt a sense of dread; the dogs were their family. And with all the recent turmoil in their lives, he worried everything could break apart if the dogs were lost forever.

The heartfelt conversation between the two fathers was interrupted by the shouting of Annie, who was running in their direction.

"Dad, dad, dad!"

"What is it, honey?" asked Mr. Keller.

She had tears in her eyes. "Joey found something. Hurry!"

Annie took off towards the river. The two men followed her. Eventually, they all landed at the shoreline, where

Joey was sitting against a log. Milton's head rested in the young boy's lap as he cried.

"What's wrong, son?" asked Mitchell.

Joey sat motionless as droplets of rain pelted his face, blending in with the tears.

Mr. Keller asked again, "Please tell me what's wrong, Joey?"

Instead of answering, Joey slowly lifted a shiny object from his pocket. It was Robin's collar.

"They're gone," Joey wept. "Robin and Summer are gone."

Chapter 14
The Den

Drip. Drip. Drip.

The cold, damp dogs knew they would not be fully dry anytime soon. The beginning scatters of rain fell upon them, further wetting their coats. It wouldn't be long before an inevitable torrential downpour.

Daylight continued to fade fast too, and the overcast did not help. Compared to the previous night, Robin and Summer were deep into the woods now. The chances of finding safe shelter were slim. Still, they trekked on in search of somewhere to camp. They also wanted to get away from the river and the fox as much as possible.

In their search, they noticed giant paw tracks leading toward the river. The prints were larger than a fox's, even bigger than the print of a human hand. They were imprinted deep into the mud, leaving spotted holes along a dirt trail.

They had no time to dwell. The dogs traversed an upward slope of hills to the north. If they could reach higher ground, they would have a better view of locating shelter. The trees were taller in this area, so it was difficult to spot the mountain they were using as their guide.

An echo of rolling thunder boomed across the forest. The rain started to pick up into a drizzle. Both their paws were caked with mud, creating a more challenging climb towards the top of the incline, they gazed across the land. All they saw were trees, trees, and more trees.

Eventually, they caught a glimpse of the mountain, but the density of the forest still blocked a complete view. Flocks of birds fled their nests as the storm drew nearer.

Another sound of thunder was followed by a bolt of lightning as the dogs reached the top of the hill. The lightning struck close to where the dogs were walking. In a split decision, Robin and Summer picked up the pace and headed down the other side of the hill. They thought it was best to descend during a thunderstorm. As rare as that was, getting struck by lightning needed to be avoided. That would be something they would have no chance of surviving.

The dogs were running out of time to find shelter, and the slippery nature of the mud created difficulties for the climb down. Robin ignored this, and the result was terrible.

Mudslide!

Robin moved too quickly. He lost his footing and fell into Summer below him. The two repeatedly tumbled, causing them to get caught in a muddy avalanche. Moments later, they crashed into a sprawling pile of leaves, branches, and pine cones, nearly striking a tree.

The two annoyed dogs emerged from the pile, plastered in mud, twigs, and crunched leaves. Summer's face had planted itself into the mound first, resulting in more dirt on her face. Her eyesight was already below average, but now her face was covered in mud, and she couldn't see. While she tried to wipe off the mud unsuccessfully, Robin spotted something curious.

It was a cavern burrowed deep within the next nearby

rolling hill. Dark brambles and dead vines covered the entrance of the eerie dirt cave.

Only one goal remained in Robin's mind: to find shelter. He licked some dirt off Summer's face, helping free the mud from her eyes. She, too, spotted the gaping hole in the hill a few yards away. Like her brother, she wanted shelter terribly. This appeared to be their best solution.

Robin ran ahead, stopping short outside the entrance. His nose, though still scratched, caught a new scent. Meanwhile, Summer spotted giant footprints exiting the cavern. They were similar in size to the ones they saw leading to the river, though another set of two was slightly smaller. These smaller prints were fresh.

The rain tapered off as they slowly approached the cave entrance. With each step closer, they could hear a rumbling growl that echoed inside the cave. And then two shadowy figures crawled toward them.

It wasn't a cave. The dogs realized they were breaching a bear's den.

The two black bears, a male and a female, emerged. Their stature was small; clearly, there were cubs. They still outsized the pups significantly, both in height and weight. Their movements were clumsy and uncoordinated.

Tired, wet, and aware of no escape, the dogs were shocked. Summer and Robin remained locked in fear.

The female bear cub walked toward them, but Robin and Summer remained glued. She began circling the dogs, sniffing their presence. Despite the small frames of Robin and Summer, the cub wondered if they were up to no good.

The male cub followed the same procedure, eyeing the dogs as he stood on his hind legs. The cubs' inspection of Summer and Robin went on for a minute or so, and all along, the dogs didn't move a muscle or blink an eye. The cubs' hot breaths wafted as they sniffed the dogs up and down.

The dogs had a choice. Should they try to escape by running for it, or should they accept the ugly fate of being the bears' next meal? Before they could decide, the male club began shaking a stick playfully. He shook it so excitedly that he fell back on his butt. He then rolled playfully on his back, wagging the stick. He made a noise that sounded like laughter. To the dogs' disbelief, the cub initiated a friendship; he wanted to play.

The female cub licked the faces of Robin and Summer, grinning at them with amusement. She then ran back into the den and rolled out a desecrated beehive. Inside the hive was a mixture of thick, delicious honey. The bear pawed a scoop and ate some; her brother pawed an even larger scoop and devoured a golden glob of the sticky treat. His snout and black-crested lips were swamped with honey.

The sister cub pushed the hive to Robin and Summer. It was an offer of food. The dogs hesitantly began licking the hive's inner combs, eating up the sweet honey. It was their first meal since receiving kibble from Whisper the day before.

The honey tasted rich and sweet; the dogs licked the combs feverishly. The taste was heavenly, and the hunger was gone. It reminded the dogs of the few times Annie and Joey would sneak some of their favorite sweets and snacks under the kitchen table, such as peanut butter or whipped cream.

The bears were no threat; they were incredibly friendly!

Robin and the brother cub played a game of tug of war with the stick while Summer and the sister cub took turns eating from the hive of honey. Summer joined in on the tug-of-war game when there was nearly nothing to eat, as did the sister cub. The four played together without worry, all but forgetting the rain.

The sister cub ran and jumped into a leaf pile; Summer gleefully joined. The brother cub consumed the rest of the honey hive and began rolling around on his back from the fullness. Robin mimicked the brother cub, rolling around on his back and onto his front, believing it to be a fun game.

The four new friends played together at the beginning of the evening. Weirdly enough, playing with the bear cubs reminded Robin and Summer of the joys of playing with Annie and Joey. They wished they could be here to join in the fun.

The sister club then initiated heading inside the den before the storm picked up again. Robin and Summer followed behind the brother cub when they heard loud crunches.

They then heard a more profound and threatening growl. And then a resounding roar.

The dogs turned around, as did the sibling cubs, to see a towering black bear standing defiantly on her haunches. It was the cubs' mother. The mother bear stared down at the two canine intruders with glaring concern. She was far less welcoming than her offspring.

She landed down on all fours, trembling the ground beneath the pups. Again, they stood frozen. It became clear she was not enjoying the surprise of seeing two unfamiliar creatures attempting to take up residence in her home. Her aggressive demeanor was coupled with a menacing look in her dark eyes.

In the mother cub's mouth was a dead salmon. She must have been at the river hunting, leading Robin and Summer to realize the oversized prints they saw earlier belonged to her. The question now was if she was still hungry.

The mother bear did not view the dogs as a threat to herself. They were way too small. Her concern was purely for the cubs.

Knowing why their mother was not happy, instinctively, both cubs stationed themselves side-by-side with Robin and Summer. They lovingly nuzzled the dogs and bared their jowls at their mother with resistance. This confused the mother bear – she took a step closer.

The sibling cubs moved to position themselves in front of the dogs. Thus, blocking Summer and Robin from their mother's trajectory. Nevertheless, they did their best to communicate that the small dogs were friends, not threats.

The mother cub eased her tension and threatening pose. She still eyed the little dogs carefully, but the situation was clear, these dogs must be lost. She let out a grunt to signal her approval of Robin and Summer.

Both cubs then tore into the salmon as if they didn't

just inhale mounds of honey. Robin and Summer fed from the scraps.

As all four finished the final course of their dinner, the night finally took to the sky. The mother bear, still sitting and watching cautiously, motioned both cubs and the dogs to follow her into the den.

The den space was barren primarily, except for the tatters of makeshift forest debris used as sleeping beds. There was a large one for the mother bear and two small clusters for the cubs. All three took to their positions while Robin and Summer stood by awkwardly, unsure of where they should sleep.

They were about to lie on the cold ground when the brother cub scooped up Robin and placed him in a spot within his bed. The sister bear maneuvered her body to free up space for Summer. Both dogs nestled into their sleeping areas, welcoming the warmth of the bears' thick fur. It helped stave off the dampness of their coats and the cold air from the rainstorm. The mother bear acknowledged and accepted the arrangements. Soon the group was fast asleep as the storm continued through the night.

Chapter 15
Wisdom and Wilderness

Joey and Annie cried the entire drive back to camp. At one point, they started to argue and insult each other. Then it turned into a volley of petty insults, such as who was more immature and imbecilic.

Mrs. Keller had to intervene, nicely asking them to stop. The kids ignored her plea, but she didn't ask again. She didn't want to yell. Both she and Mitch knew the kids' behavior was influenced by tiredness, agony, and hopelessness. It was situational, not personal.

Everyone at Wilderness World Camp was asleep except for Martha. She awaited the arrival of the Keller minivan while Boomer slumbered next to her chair in the main cabin house.

When the Kellers arrived, Martha invited Mitch and Fran to stay at the camp instead of heading back to their dingy hotel miles away. The tired couple took her up on the offer.

Although the guest cabin accommodations were superb, Mitchell and Francine remained awake with the kids. Exhausted from the long day of searching for Summer and Robin, the Kellers' minds were racing with thoughts – sleep was not an option.

The immense despair hovering over the Keller family weighed heavy as they sat together at the kitchen table. The thunderstorm had picked up. Everything outside was soaking wet.

"They're probably drenched," said Annie. "I hope they found shelter."

Joey scoffed, rolling his tired eyes. "They didn't find shelter. They are dead, Annie. They died in that river."

Annie hit her brother's good arm, the one without the cast. "Don't say that! Just shut up! You were better off being silent. You never have anything positive to say."

Joey snapped back, "You know it's true! Stop being an idiot."

Annie took another shot at her brother. Joey motioned to retaliate, but Mr. Keller caught his arm mid-swing.

"Stop with the name-calling, and do not hit each other," bellowed Mr. Keller. "Fighting is not the answer."

"Then what is the answer?" retorted Joey as tears streaked down the young boy's face.

Mitchell put his hand on his son's shoulder, but Joey pulled away.

"What is the answer, Dad?" repeated Joey.

Mitchell said nothing. Feeling rejected, he walked away.

Joey turned angry. "Even if you had an answer, I wouldn't listen."

Mitchell was doing all he could to keep his cool, he understood why his son was upset, but Joey was pushing things way too far.

Joey lashed out again.

"By tomorrow night, everyone in this room will admit the dogs are lost forever. And then, on the drive home, you and mom will promise Annie and me that we'll get replacement dogs if we pull A's again in school this year. But the problem is we did that last year, and the reward was you and mom losing our dogs. So the answer is we got those awesome grades for nothing! We busted our butts for nothing because our dogs are dead!"

Annie stood from her chair. She yelled at her brother, "No, they are not dead! They are in the woods, and they are alive. I know it!"

Joey stood up and got in her face, yelling even louder, "Give me a break Annie. How are two small house dogs the size of puppies to survive in the woods?"

Annie answered, "They are tough; they can do it."

"Annie, you're delusional," Joey said. "You saw the huge paw prints at the river, don't pretend you didn't. The prints were bear tracks. You think Summer and Robin are any match against a hungry bear?"

Annie started to cry.

Joey doubled down on his remarks. "Look at the facts. The dogs are alone in a dark, rainy forest without food or water. They either drowned in the river, or they were eaten by a bear. And let's not overlook this little piece of evidence."

Joey held Robin's collar in the air, then tossed it on the kitchen table. Every Keller looked down at the collar. Annie sunk her face into her hands.

Annie and Joey had their moments of sibling arguments, but none equaled this. There was scorn in their voices, and they could no longer look at each other. The animosity carried over toward their parents too.

"Joey, I'm confident they are alive," said Mrs. Keller softly. "Those dogs are tougher than they look. Verona believes they are alive, as does Felix. Your dad believes it too."

Mr. Keller nodded in agreement, but he wasn't very convincing. While Mitch believed the dogs were alive, his expression conveyed doubts. The likelihood of survival after two days and nights in the woods was considerably low. Finding Robin's collar by the river only confirmed his suspicions even more. And he, too, saw the bear tracks but said nothing in hopes the kids had not. Clearly, he was wrong.

Mitchell knew, as did Fran, they would have to prepare the children to deal with the grief and loss of losing their beloved dogs. But, he recalled the advice of Felix; it was time to strengthen the Keller bond by healing together.

"When Zoey died, we didn't blame each other or carry guilt, rightfully so. But, in the case of Summer and Robin, losing them feels different because we are at fault. The guilt is taking hold of us all, and blame is tossed around the table. This makes everyone sad and angry, which is why you're both bickering and crying every two minutes. It's got to stop," explained Mitchell.

Mrs. Keller nodded in agreement. "Your father and I love those dogs too. We may not be crying like you, but believe me, we're hurting inside. Fighting and yelling result in nothing and crying will negatively cloud your thoughts. We all need to be positive, and we need to work together as a team."

Annie lashed out. "Are you kidding me, mom? Your words are totally hypocritical. You and dad have been fighting nonstop long before you lost Summer and Robin. You've been at each other's throats for months, so don't make it like you guys are shining examples of how to deal with conflict."

Joey said, "We haven't felt like a family in a long time. Right now, you're putting on an act; you're pretending to be a team in front of all the campers. If anybody is breaking our family bond, it's the two of you."

Annie added, "And mom, how dare you preach about crying? I can't count how many times I've seen you run off to the bedroom with teary eyes after arguments with dad."

She continued, "I saw you crying your eyes out last month after dad mentioned getting a divorce. And then, two days later, you are shipping us off to camp."

Joey's face turned white. "Oh my God, are you getting a divorce?"

The Keller parents looked at each other. Everything was coming to a head, and they were unprepared for the conversation.

Mitch had mentioned the possibility of divorce, but he didn't think the kids heard the comment. More importantly, it was said during an argument one night. Neither he nor Fran wanted to break up.

"Annie, you are one hundred percent correct. We've been arguing for months. The dogs are lost because your mom and I were distracted; we weren't seeing eye-to-eye in the car. But we are not putting on an act; we are doing the best we can considering the circumstances."

"If it's not an act, answer this question: do you still love mom?" asked Joey.

"Yes! I love your mom to the moon and back, and I do not want a divorce," said Mitchell as he walked over to his wife. "Sometimes adults say stupid things they don't mean."

Mitchell needed to show the kids he was being honest.

"Francine, you are my soulmate. I love you and want to be your husband until my last day on earth. I am so sorry for the past few months."

Mrs. Keller began to tear up. "I'm sorry too, Mitch. I will love you forever."

The Keller parents kissed and embraced tighter than they ever had before. Within a few seconds, all four Kellers were hugging as a group.

Knowing their mom and dad would remain married made the heaviness much lighter. The family had hit rock bottom, but it was time to bounce back up.

Annie turned to her brother. "Joey, how much do you want to bet I will find the dogs before you do?"

"Annie, I'll think positive and go with your hunch about them being alive. So I'll take your bet because if Summer and Robin are alive, I will find them first," responded Joey.

Mr. Keller smiled. "That's the attitude we need!"

~

It was dawn. Streaks of violet and blue sky mixed with the fading of gray clouds. The sunrise brightened the dark bear den, forcing the slumbering Robin and Summer to awaken.

It had been a long night, starting with a thunderstorm that raged on for hours. The deafening sounds kept the dogs and cubs restless. Sometimes it sounded as if the lightning was striking right next to them.

The end of the thunderstorm made room for a full moon. And with it came a new set of noises, mainly howling, specifically from neighboring wolves.

The bears didn't flinch; they heard the wolves every night. But the dogs were highly anxious. These types of evil sounds were foreign to them. And to make matters worse, the dogs knew they couldn't stay in the bear den forever.

When morning arrived, Robin and Summer were exhausted. At best, they slept for two hours. Even so, it was time to get going. So they stood up and stretched their little bodies. Meanwhile, the cubs and mama bear were up and ready to go. They were headed for a journey to the river.

Despite Robin and Summer being anxious to find the Keller family, the dogs were excited about having breakfast by the river. They knew it would be wise to put food in their bellies before moving on. Plus, they felt relaxed and safe knowing the bears were with them if the fox reappeared.

The morning was spent with the dogs learning the methods of catching salmon. It was all about timing. The mama bear effortlessly captured scores of fish, tossing them to the shoreline of the riverbank.

While not as talented as her mother, the sister cub was still quite impressive in her fishing skills. She caught a few salmon, even snagging one at the gills with the snap of her teeth. Her brother, meanwhile, had no grace in his method. He was clumsy with barely any calculation; he struggled to catch a single fish. His loud splashing sent many of them darting away. At some point, he tired out and began eating the catch from his sister's pile.

Robin and Summer attempted to mimic the bears' methods, careful enough not to slip into the river's tide again, though they did rinse themselves off. They needed to eliminate all the grime and mud covering their bodies.

The dogs tried submerging their faces into the water to bite and snag a slippery salmon. But the pink fish was quicker than they anticipated.

Eventually, the dogs managed to catch a few, impressing the mama bear. It was the first time they ever caught their own food and the first time eating fish. Although they weren't crazy about the taste, they preferred the steak Joey would offer during Sunday family dinners!

They were finishing breakfast together when Robin and Summer heard the owl hooting again. Something told them it was time to continue forward in their journey.

Using nudges, nods, and face licks, the dogs bid goodbye to the bears and headed north.

As the woods were drying from the rising morning sun, the dogs went to the bathroom in the dewy grass before continuing the trek north. But then reality hit them – they were unsure which direction to take. They listened closely again for the hooting.

Hoooot, hoot.

The yellow eyes of the great-horned owl glared overhead at the two dogs from a towering oak tree. He let out another series of hoots. No doubt Robin and Summer knew this owl – it was their protector from the night in Milton's doghouse.

Why was the owl following them?

The dogs were confused, wondering if the owl was trying to tell them something. A sense of wisdom radiated with the owl's being; its stoic nature portrayed a sense of guidance and security. Maybe the owl wanted the dogs to *follow him.*

The owl flew from its perch toward a different oak tree a few yards north. It turned its head full one-hundred-and-eighty degrees, now staring at the dogs again. Robin and Summer understood the hint – they would follow his path.

As they reached the tree base, the owl took flight. He traveled a bit, eventually landing on another tree due north. The dogs followed.

When they arrived at the owl's new tree location, they could catch a glimpse of the mountain again. It was looming in the north, the same direction as the owl's flight path.

The owl was leading the dogs somewhere, but only the bird knew the final destination. Civilization, maybe? With little sense of direction or options, Summer and Robin followed the owl's lead, hoping they made the right decision.

Chapter 16
Night Terrors

Joey and Annie decided to stay with their parents in the guest cabin. After hours of arguing, they all settled their differences with apologies and promises of finding the dogs. It was nearly midnight by the time the Keller family went to bed.

Joey was deep asleep when his night terrors resurfaced...

"It's time to go. We need to get Zoey."

The Keller family was in the minivan. It was only a fifteen-minute drive, but it felt like an eternity. Rain fell down hard, thumping on the windshield. Thunder and lightning filled the sky.

The gray brick building stood like a pillar of doom. There were no other cars in the parking lot.

The parents walked through the double doors of the building. Then Annie. Then Joey. A nurse stood waiting for them.

"This way," said the nurse. She pointed to a hallway that had no end.

They followed her through a narrow, cobweb-infested corridor littered with abandoned crates, empty food and water bowls, and rotten chew toys. Everything felt so sad and cold.

The nurse opened the doors to a dimly lit room. A

table rested in its center. On it was a body draped over by a dark plastic cover. Joey knew by the outline the body underneath the plastic was Zoey's.

A sharp pain ran through his chest as the nurse lifted the cover. Mrs. Keller started to cry; Annie cried too. His dad had to look away. But Joey stared at the lifeless body. He couldn't take his eyes off her.

She was motionless. No movement. No breathing. Her soft coat was now static and coarse. Her eyes were closed. Her ears drooped.

"No!" cried Joey. "Zoey can't be dead."

Joey went to hug her. Hoping the hug would bring her back to life. He closed his eyes tight and prayed. He then looked to Heaven and begged for another chance. Hoping his prayers had been answered, he looked down at the table. The situation had changed. Zoey was no longer the dog on the table. It was Summer.

"No, no, no!" screamed Joey.

He rubbed his eyes, hoping he was seeing it all wrong. It couldn't be Summer.

He looked away, turning to his parents and Annie. Their faces looked blank.

He turned back to the table. Summer was gone. Now it was Robin's lifeless body.

"What is happening?!" asked Joey.

"Robin is gone," said the nurse. "Summer is gone too."

Joey hollered at the nurse, "No, they can't be dead! You're lying!"

The nurse stood firm, "They're gone. And it's because of you and your family."

"No, no, no, no...."

Joey woke with a loud gasp, trying to catch his breath. His clothes and bedsheets were drenched in sweat. He looked at his watch. It was two o'clock in the morning. He calmed himself down. It was just another nightmare. But then sadness overcame him.

After quietly changing his pajamas, Joey attempted to lie back down and return to sleep. A few minutes passed, and then he entered a rhythm of rest, uninterrupted.

Meanwhile, Annie lay in the other cot, completely awake. Joey shouting the dog's name in his sleep woke her. His nightmares were getting worse. And she knew the only thing that would solve his nightmares would be finding Robin and Summer.

Annie remained awake in her bed, plotting how the search would unfold in a few hours. She asked herself a series of questions. *Where should we look first? Are both dogs alive, or is Robin gone forever?*

She knew that if Summer was found alive, but Robin was not, Joey's nightmares would never go away. *Would Joey ever recover?*

The clock read 5:15. The morning was just beginning, but Joey and his parents were sleeping soundly. Annie was wide awake. Unfortunately, despite all those hours of staring at the ceiling, she couldn't find the answers to her questions. Maybe she was too tired, or perhaps she was over-thinking. Either way, she knew the sun would be rising soon; she needed to get some sleep before it did.

Annie slowly closed her eyes as one final thought ran through her head: She thought of how the day ahead would be the most challenging day of her life.

Chapter 17
A Group Effort

A series of knocks pattered at the front door of the Keller cabin. Joey and Annie were already awake and out of their cots, readying themselves to begin another day searching for Robin and Summer.

Mrs. Keller was brewing coffee while Mr. Keller was showering. Still, in her nightgown, she answered the door. Standing there, to her surprise, was Edwin and a group of campers.

"Good morning Mrs. Keller!" chimed Edwin.

"Good morning, Ed," answered Mrs. Keller.

"Are Annie and Joey around?" asked Kirsten. She was holding something covered in a red blanket. It was something rectangular, possibly a picture frame.

"Yes, let me go get them."

Mrs. Keller convened to the kitchen where Annie and Joey were chowing down on cereal. "A few of your friends are at the door looking for you two. Why don't you greet them while I get dressed."

Joey and Annie met the campers at the front door. Kirsten and Emily were standing front and center, with several other campers behind them. They smiled gleefully, holding their surprise with impatience.

"We know how upset you are about Robin and Summer," said Kirsten.

She unwrapped the rectangular object in her hand. "Emily and I made this last night for you."

It was a framed portrait of Robin and Summer, a detailed sketch made in colored pencil. The details were spot on. The portrait showcased them standing together in front of a lake. The dogs looked happy in the picture.

"It's beautiful," said Annie. "Thank you."

She hugged both Kirsten and Emily. Then Joey's friend Austin and his little brother Oliver stepped forward with a brown bag.

"We wanted to help your family search for the dogs today," said Austin. "Edwin took us to the pet store; we grabbed doggy treats and a few whistles."

"Don't forget the cowbell," chimed Edwin.

Austin pulled an old silver cowbell out of the bag and rang it with all his might. The sound loudly echoed through the cabin.

"Wow, that's loud," said Mr. Keller as he entered the foyer. "What's going on here?"

"They've come to help with the search," said Joey, also showing him the Robin and Summer portrait. "There's no time to waste."

"Mom and I will take our coffees to go," said Mr. Keller.

Within the group was Boomer, who was known for his keen sense of smell.

"Boomer is great at finding things; he can help with the search," said Kirsten. "My dad said we can also use the ATV to cover more ground."

Edwin entered the cabin and displayed his paper map of the woods across the kitchen table.

"We'll start scouting by the woods outside the gardens and then bridge over to the hiking trails. Let's always use the buddy system, and don't stray too far off the perimeter. And under no circumstance can we allow the kids to go deep into the woods."

Austin rang the cowbell once. Mr. Keller grimaced and drew his hand to cup his ear. It was the last sound on earth an adult would want to hear before having his morning coffee.

Edwin asked, "Joey and Annie, are you two ready?"

The siblings smiled. They were anxious to get going.

"Let's find Summer and Robin," said Joey.

Mrs. Keller emerged from the bedroom, fully dressed in hiking gear. Mr. Keller handed her a coffee to go. He whispered to his wife, "That cowbell will drive me crazy, but if it doesn't help find the dogs, nothing will."

Fran chuckled at the little joke but turned very serious with her own comment. "Mitch, the more I think about it, the more I fear we will find the dogs. Only they will be seriously hurt, or even worse. What do we do if that happens?"

Mitchell responded, "I don't have an answer for you, Francine, but if we find them, odds are it will turn out badly."

Chapter 18
The Pit

Robin and Summer followed the wise owl's trajectory through the woods. His pace was slow enough for the dogs to keep up, though the mystery of where the owl was headed kept them cautious. They moved forward with a hint of hesitation.

On the opposing end, what if the owl was leading them into a trap? On a positive note, could the owl lead them to some kind of dog-friendly sanctuary? There was no way to decipher a direct answer, but the owl had been an ally so far. So, the dogs' only choice was to follow the owl, trust their instincts, and remain cautious.

Sometimes when the owl flew to a faraway tree, he would let out a series of hoots for the dogs to keep track of his whereabouts. It was difficult to follow him. The forest surroundings would change frequently. Some areas were thick and condensed with trees, but others were wide open fields.

The owl swooped under a sprawl of branches; he was out of sight. Robin and Summer rushed forward as fast as they could to catch up until they ran into thick, high grass bushes. Their pursuit was interrupted; the dogs barreled through the brush as best as they could.

Summer paused momentarily, letting out a sneeze from the airborne pollen. Robin exited the brush first. He saw what lay before them. It was eye-opening and exhilarating. A large, swathing, green valley.

Summer and Robin stood in amazement. There were no trees, just short grass and rolling hills for as far as their eyes could see. Fields of violet lavender plants were flourishing in patches throughout the terrain. It was heavenly.

Excited to trek ahead, the dogs leaped into a run-hop rhythm, basking in the beauty of the landscape. They saw the owl again, flying effortlessly about halfway across the valley.

Nature was thriving. Bumble bees buzzed routinely from flower to flower, petal to petal. A stray rabbit raced east across the green grass, passing mole hills and ant nests along the way. Blue jays and robins whistled as they flew across the light blue sky. Periodically a butterfly or two would appear. This place felt safe.

Robin stopped at a tiny quarry of stones and examined an intricate spider web, its entire composure perfect and untainted. The web's owner, a yellow garden spider, diligently spun a cocoon around its caught prey – a sapphire-colored mud wasp.

Summer meanwhile frolicked into the lavender meadows. She was sneezy, but her fascination with the flowers overpowered her allergies. A stray ladybug landed on her nose; she sneezed, and it went buzzing away, joining the swarm of flying bugs embellishing the plants.

The owl gave off a series of hoots, interrupting the distracted dogs. Summer and Robin reconvened, realizing it was time to move on.

They continued across the valley to follow the owl. He was a blip at this point toward the opposite edge of the valley, so they turned their run into a sprint. Along the way, they passed mosquitoes and mice in the grassy field. They also saw frogs sitting on pads in a small pond. What they failed to recognize was the big shadow looming directly above them.

Suddenly, everything changed for Robin and Summer. The pretty chimes of nature were interrupted by a screeching caw. The sound was deafening and frightening. Robin halted and turned to see Summer. She was barking madly as she was lifted airborne by her collar. The culprit was a giant, fierce, northern goshawk with a wing span of nearly seventy inches.

In a flash, Summer was lifted about three feet into the air. Then ten feet. The dog was heavier than the hawk had estimated, but the hawk was hungry – very hungry.

Summer was soaring well off the ground at about fifteen feet. Robin chased the monstrous bird who kidnapped his sister. Summer hovered over Robin as the hawk's talon snared firmly around her collar. Robin needed to act fast; the hawk's tight grip around the collar was choking his sister.

Robin barked with all his might, chasing after the hawk and attempting to leap high into the air to snatch his sister. But she was too far above the ground. Robin feared the giant bird would soar away at a pace that was impossible to track. But the hawk struggled to elevate and couldn't fly very fast because of Summer's weight.

The hawk flapped its wings excessively to achieve

additional lift. Summer was dangling in mid-air. Robin prayed she didn't fall – a drop from that height could kill her. But so too would the collar choking her; so too would the hawk who wanted Summer for a meal. The situation was dire.

Robin continued to follow after the hawk. Desperation coursed through him. He refused to lose his sister to some pesky hawk.

At twenty feet, the hawk was struggling to hold Summer. But the thought of losing his meal was enough to inspire the hawk to find his next level of strength. The bird flapped its vast wings with incredible ferocity; he was determined to return to his nest. It would only be a moment or two before he could enjoy his hefty meal.

Another swooping shadow emerged overhead. Robin looked up to see the owl! He had flown to the rescue.

With his talons flared, the owl repeatedly struck at the hawk to free Summer. The chokehold from the collar was tightening, making it difficult to breathe. Summer started to lose consciousness.

The commotion continued as both birds traveled across the valley's sky. Robin was towing behind as fast as he could. The hawk attempted to swoop down to avoid the owl, but he pursued diligently. The owl knew Summer had no more than a few seconds remaining.

With a two-strike combo using his talons, the owl critically injured the hawk – causing it to screech.

The hawk couldn't battle the owl and hold Summer simultaneously, so he flew down to a lower elevation. His plan was to trap and keep Summer in a feeding spot, like a deep ditch, for later after his fight with the owl. But the hawk had to ensure Summer would not escape, so the hawk tightened its grip on her collar. A dead meal would have no chance of running away.

Summer gasped for air but continued to choke. She went limp as Robin barked like a maniac, fearing his sister was dying in front of him. With the hawk just ten feet off the ground, the owl rammed into the nasty predator again. The collision caused Summer's collar to rip. Summer was now in freefall.

Robin, only a short distance behind them, sprinted to her quick descent. He was prepared to use his body as a landing pillow, but there was no way he would make it in time.

Instead of hitting the ground, Summer fell into a clump of bramble. But the bramble collapsed inward, sending Summer slipping into the earth.

The owl continued its attack. Now free from its prey, the hawk fought back with countless strikes at the owl. The hawk was exhausted, but the battle continued high into the sky. Neither bird would give in.

Robin paid no attention to the fight; his concern was Summer. He darted to the rim of the pit Summer tumbled into and peered down to find her below.

The pit was layered with dirt edges that spiraled down into the earth. That is where Robin spotted Summer. She was on one of the last edges towards the bottom. His sister was alive but seriously wounded, wincing in pain over her right hind leg.

Robin saw something else at the very bottom of the pit. It was the most frightening, terrifying sight he had encountered during this unexpected adventure. And undoubtedly, what Robin saw presented grave danger to his sister.

Chapter 19
Cowbell Calls

Ding-ding-ding-ding-ding!

Austin shook the cowbell with all his might. The sound of bells echoed throughout the forest. Mr. Keller plugged his ears.

"I think everyone in the state can hear the cowbell," joked Mr. Keller.

"Guess that means everyone will know to look for Robin and Summer," Mrs. Keller joked back.

The Kellers and all the campers, including Edwin and Martha, were determined to search every crevice. They started by checking around the campground gardens and the thorny bushes along the dirt road entrance to the camp, but there was no sign of the dogs. After a few hours, they decided to go deeper into the hiking trails, which led closer to the river.

Edwin passed by everyone on the ATV, driving in a zigzag across the manmade trails. Hoping hikers would help in the search by keeping a lookout, Edwin stapled the remaining flyers of Robin and Summer to various trees. The handouts provided two photos of the dogs captioned *LOST*. Mrs. Keller's phone number was listed at the bottom.

The campers split up into subgroups to cover more ground. Annie was joined by Kirsten and Emily, while Joey searched with Austin and his younger brother, Oliver.

Mr. and Mrs. Keller were together with Martha and Boomer in tow. Other campers had split into groups of threes and fours. This helped cover as much ground as possible.

A few campers doubted the dogs would be near the perimeter. The dogs were lost for so many days, so they must have gone deep into the forest. And if they went deep within, there was no way they'd survive.

Joey and Annie could hear the whispers of concern, but they blocked out the naysayers. Instead, they focused on hope. It's the only thing they had going for them.

Drowning out the negative comments wasn't all too easy sometimes during the search. For example, Annie wasn't thrilled about Emily mentioning when her family lost her pet lizard, Buster.

According to Emily, her family spent days looking everywhere around the house for Buster. However, it wasn't until a week later they found the tiny lizard crushed in the backyard. Apparently, a cat got to him but did not like the taste. Emily went on to say they put Buster in a shoe box and buried him next to the swing set.

It was a strange story to tell, considering the circumstances. Annie shut the story down by interrupting Emily; Annie began yelling at the top of her lungs: "Robin... Summer... Robin... Summer!"

Everyone joined in. All the campers and Kellers called out the names *Summer and Robin*. Their voices echoed through the forest. Austin chimed his cowbell over and over again. If Robin and Summer were within a mile's distance, they would unquestionably hear the voices and noises.

The group made noise and called out for around twenty minutes. And yet, still no sign of Robin or Summer.

"Thank you, Austin, for helping me," said Joey. "I know it's not how you wanted to spend your day. But my sister and I really appreciate it."

Austin patted him on the back. "That's what friends are for. Plus, I think we'll find your dogs before the girls do. I even made a bet with Kirsten that we would find them first. And we will."

The boys high-fived each other. They were ahead of the other groups, dredging deeper into one of the southbound hiking trails that cut through a range of oak trees. Edwin drove up to them on the ATV.

"This thing is running low on gas," said Edwin. "I'm heading back to the garage. I don't want you guys going deeper into the woods – do not go further than the perimeter I outlined on the map."

The boys acknowledged Edwin's warning, and he sped off on the ATV. However, Joey didn't care about the perimeter or where it ended; he went deeper to find his dogs. Austin and Oliver followed his lead.

Oliver tugged on his brother's shirt.

"I am afraid of bears; maybe we should go back."

Austin responded, "Bears won't hurt us if we make a lot of noise."

Austin gave the cowbell a thunderous ring – but Joey wished he hadn't because he could have sworn he heard something right before the chime. Something far into the distance. It was hard to tell with the ATV's engine echoing through the forest, but Joey was certain he heard a bark.

"Did you hear that?" asked Joey.

"The cowbell? Who hasn't?" answered Oliver rhetorically. Austin fist-bumped his brother's shoulder.

"No, not the cowbell. I think I heard barking," said Joey. But before he could elaborate, Annie ran up to their group, beaming with happiness and anxiety.

"Joey, I think I heard the dogs," exclaimed Annie. "I think I heard Robin and Summer!"

Chapter 20
Holding On

Robin helplessly watched as a collection of copperhead snakes slithered at the bottom of the pit.

Summer was injured and unmoving.

She groaned with pain in the depths of the pit filled with venomous serpents. It was hard to count just how many there were due to their entangling bodies. It was an interweaving sphere of at least a dozen snakes, maybe more.

Robin growled.

One of the snakes made its way toward Summer, lying on the ridge a few feet above the pit's bottom. She was dazed from her fall, but Robin's growl alerted her to the dangerous situation.

Summer had a pink and purple snake toy at the Keller household that squeaked when she would bite it. The toy was harmless and cute; it was one of the first gifts Annie gave Summer on their adoption day. It's been her favorite toy ever since.

The creature in front of Summer looked nothing like her toy. It was a sinister serpent, its eyes dark as death itself.

The five-foot snake slithered in an *S* formation, perking its forked tongue in twitchy motions. Its reflective black eyes stared directly at Summer. One bite from a copperhead is enough to paralyze a large dog like Milton. But Summer was a small dog facing an entire army of snakes. One bite, let alone multiple bites, could be fatal.

The snake's attention was fixed on Summer. It was roughly a foot away from her. Summer remained still as a statue. She was too terrified to make any sudden movements or noises. Despite her painful injuries, she stopped moaning. The only noise coming from the pit was the sound of hissing.

The other snakes below were still writhing amongst themselves, not paying attention to Summer. One wrong move could alert them to her presence. She was petrified. She didn't know what to do about the snakes below, and she was near breathless over the slithering serpent that was now twelve inches from her face.

Even if Summer had a plan, her ability to move was limited by her injury and a lack of space – Summer was stuck.

Robin acted fast; he searched for anything to help his sister escape the pit. He spotted something only a few feet away. Summer's ripped collar. He was uncertain if it would be long enough, but he would try his best.

Scooping the collar up with his mouth, he brought the broken strap to the pit's edge. He tried to lower the collar down as much as possible to Summer. But, as he predicted, it was way too short.

Robin went on the search again. This time he found a stick about four feet in length. He bit into one end and brought it over to the pit. That's when a big problem presented itself to Robin; lowering the stick to Summer would trigger the snake. Robin retreated. He needed a distraction.

Not far from where he found the stick was the corpse

of a field mouse. He felt terrible about using one of the mouse's bodies as bait, but his options were limited.

Robin nabbed the dead mouse's tail with his teeth. He ran to the pit and launched the little creature into the darkness below. The snake that had been focused on Summer changed its focus to the dead mouse. It slivered down into the mesh of snakes, joining the fight for the chance to gobble up the little meal.

With the snakes distracted, Robin lowered the stick to Summer. She gradually tried to snap at its end but to no avail. The effort caused her to moan – the throbbing pain in her injured leg intensified.

Robin repeated the process. He tried to place it near her mouth again, but it slipped from his teeth. The stick fell, landing within the sphere of snakes.

All snakes were too busy fighting over the dead mouse to notice the stick, except for the one initially hunting Summer. It slivered back towards the injured dog. Robin needed another distraction. He kicked Summer's collar into the pit. It hit the evil snake on the head before falling deeper into the army of serpents.

The snake was unhappy with the collar hit. It turned its attention skyward at Robin, realizing his foe was above the pit. The snake slivered past Summer as if she didn't exist. Then, the five-foot copperhead climbed with an eerie, predatory motion toward Robin – it was looking to confront its attacker without mercy.

As it approached the top, the snake let out a warning hiss. Robin tried to retreat a few steps but tripped and tumbled onto his back. The snake curved out of the pit and rushed toward him with his fangs glaring, ready to strike.

Robin closed his eyes, preparing for the inevitable bite. But instead, he heard a *whooshing* noise. And then a hoot.

He opened his eyes to see the owl. It had returned from its fight with the hawk, arriving again to rescue the dogs in the nick of time.

In an act of heroism, the owl scooped the snake up with its talons. The serpent wiggled rapidly in its grasp as they went airborne. The snake tried to strike the owl, but his talons pierced into its head. In an instant, the snake was dead.

Typically, the snake would make for a hearty meal for the owl. But he recognized the dogs could use it for something dire at the moment; the dead snake could help lift Summer from the pit as a rope.

The owl dropped the snake's body next to Robin, indicating he would have to do the rest of the work on his own. Robin snatched the dead snake up by its neck. He then lowered its five-foot, boneless body into the pit. It was long enough to reach his sister. It spooked Summer at first until she realized it was lifeless.

Understanding the gesture, Summer clamped onto the snake's tail. Using all his might, Robin attempted to hoist his sister up. It was the same strategy they used to escape the waterfall. Summer held on to the snake with every bit of strength she could muster.

Robin pulled, inch by inch, while Summer's climbed

up. She was hovering over the slithering snakes below. Luckily, the snake's body was thick enough to maintain the tension. But Summer's survival rested solely on Robin's agility and strength.

Summer was heavier than Robin, and pulling her up and out was getting more difficult by the second. Robin's adrenaline started to wither. He felt the dead snake slipping from his grasp. Robin had to pause to catch his breath and muster up more energy.

Summer's motion upward had stopped when she was halfway to safety. Suspended in mid-climb, she realized her brother had stopped lifting. Robin's timing was terrible. The snakes had finished devouring the mouse, and soon they would recognize Summer's presence again.

With the snake in her teeth, Summer did her best to push out a muffled growl. Robin heard his sister's warning loud and clear. This was a game of tug he had to win. With all of his might, Robin pulled Summer up the steep incline. She tried to dig her front legs into the dirt wall to maintain positioning and avoid falling back into the pit.

However, her digging into the wall sent dirt pebbles below. This irritated the army of snakes. They took action by moving towards her. One of the snakes broke away from the pack and began to slither around the edges leading up from the pit in a circular motion. The snake moved faster than Robin was pulling up his sister; the eager serpent was mere inches from Summer. She warned her brother again – she issued another muffled growl.

Robin pulled harder, but the snake had reached his

sister. It attempted to coil around Summer's hind leg but failed due to a swift paw kick by Summer. Then, using her good leg, she sent the snake flying down into the pit.

Again, the snakes were irritated. This time they all released hisses. A few snakes began ascending towards Summer.

Robin continued to pull up on the snake rope, lifting Summer higher and higher along the incline. One of the snakes attempted to strike Summer before she could escape. But the serpent miscalculated; its fangs hit the rock wall, causing it to tumble below into the pit.

Robin pulled again as Summer continued to use her front legs to climb the wall. Finally, she managed to bring her front paws over the edge.

Summer leaped over the pit with a hefty thrust of her good hind leg and tumbled into the ground, barely escaping another snake's strike. She let out a high-pitched cry; her injured leg was throbbing.

Robin was heading over to his sister when he noticed more snakes were exiting the pit. As a group, they slithered towards Summer. Tangled within the army of serpents was Summer's collar, now lying on the ground.

Robin let out a series of barks, stopping most of the snakes in their tracks. One of the copperheads ignored Robin and continued slithering toward Summer. And then it stopped.

Summer and Robin froze in place as they watched the red and brown colored serpent slowly raise its head and spread its neck open wide to resemble a striking cobra. Before Robin or Summer could react, it sprung at them.

Robin quickly positioned his body in front of Summer to shield her from the strike. Its fangs hit Robin squarely on his shoulder. The pain was sharp and alarming. Robin yelped in agony but remained vigilant. He was prepared to protect his sister, no matter how many copperheads he would have to fight.

Before the snake could strike a second time, the owl swooped in and snatched it like the other from before. This time the newly captured snake would make for his meal, eventually.

The owl put down the dead snake. It then stood guard near the pit and hooted at the remaining copperheads. This caused a much-needed distraction to allow the dogs to escape from the valley and back into the forest.

Summer limped ahead. Her leg hurt a little more with each attempt at movement. She was emotionally spent and remained petrified with fear.

Feeling the pain from the snake bite, Robin looked back and made eye contact with the owl's beautiful, wide yellow eyes. A moment of thankfulness was exchanged. Then, the owl flew away from the pit, deep into the sun-blinding sky.

Robin started to lag behind his limping sister, the escalating pain from the snake bite taking its toll.

Out of steam, Summer stopped moving forward. Robin caught up to her, and he stopped too. They both stood

still, each examining their injuries. Summer's leg was se-
verely damaged from the fall. The leg hurt from paw to hip.

As for her brother, the snake bite caused massive
swelling. Robin could no longer feel his shoulder. It was
completely numb.

Both dogs were unsure how much more of the forest
they could endure. The unforgiving environment was too
brutal for a pair of little house dogs.

A part of them wanted to roll into the ground and
never move again. Still, a more significant part of them, born
out of instinct, forced them into survival mode. Plus, for
there to be any chance of reuniting with the beloved Keller
family, they had to keep moving.

Either way, Robin and Summer needed a two-minute
break. They were injured, and they didn't know what to do
next.

They sniffed around for a spot to rest. But they were
interrupted by the far-distant sound of a ringing bell. It was
very far away but still faint enough to be heard clearly. It
sounded almost similar to the clanking of car keys or the
clinging noise of their dog tags. This was not a sound made
by the forest.

Barely able to move, the dogs did their injured best to
urgently follow the path of the sound. The echoing bell was
too difficult to pinpoint. Still, their senses told them to continue north toward the direction of the mountain.

Both dogs barked in response to the ringing bells.
They barked and barked and barked, trekking on without the
owl to guide them.

But then the sounds grew less and less. And soon, there were no bell sounds at all. The dogs lost the trail.

In addition to their hopes being broken and the pains intensifying, their throats were hoarse from all the barking. Moreover, they were increasingly getting thirsty and hungry too.

Summer could not continue on any further. She plopped herself next to a giant oak tree. Robin sat next to Summer. He was feeling lousy, but unlike his sister, he could still move. His gut wanted him to continue searching, but his heart said not to abandon Summer in the wild forest. His brain told him they would die if he didn't seek help. He was left with a difficult choice.

Robin looked into Summer's eyes. They were wet, sobby, and tired. There was no more motivation in her. He nudged his sister with his nose, but she did not respond – there was no budging Summer from her spot.

Knowing she would remain in place, Robin made the difficult decision to scout ahead without her. He had to find the origin of the chiming bells. He had to find Joey and Annie. It broke his heart, leaving Summer behind. He was fearful she might die shortly after he left, but there was no better option.

Summer closed her eyes. Robin licked her face. It was his way of saying, "I love you."

He took one last look at his beautiful sister, and then he turned away to head north. He was on his own, and he had never felt more alone. No Summer. No owl. No idea of what lay ahead.

Miles away, the owl was returning to his home nesting grounds. He was flying across the valley when he spotted the fire-red predator with raised pointy ears and a slinking nature to its prowl.

It was the fox. He looked hungry, and he was following the trail of Robin and Summer.

Chapter 21
Expert Opinion

"I swear I heard them barking!"

The Keller family sat at the picnic table outside the guest cabin. Joey was on the verge of a meltdown. His emotions had been running high the last few days, but the past couple of hours made him feel like he was losing his mind. Annie, too.

The search party had been called off for a number of reasons. One, the campers were tired out. Two, Austin, Oliver, and another camper caught rashes from poison oak. Three, the weather was taking a nasty turn. And finally, Edwin accidentally flipped over the ATV on his way back to the camp to refuel. Luckily, he only scraped up his leg and twisted an ankle; Martha was tending to him in the infirmary.

"Edwin, the ankle is probably sprained, but you'll be okay. You're lucky it's not broken," said Martha with a hint of aggravation.

"To be perfectly honest, I am lucky my neck didn't snap in half. I missed hitting my head on the tree by a matter of feet," explained Edwin.

"And now we have three campers with poison oak. What are we supposed to tell their parents? Sorry Mr. Donohue, but Austin and Oliver have poison oak because they were deep in the woods looking for someone's dogs!" remarked Martha. "We'll lose all our campers. No parent wants to hear that sort of thing."

Edwin knew she was correct. Helping the Keller family search for the dogs around the camp perimeter was one thing, but the passion everyone held for finding Summer and Robin was leading them dangerously into the deep woods.

"I saw some of the kids going too deep into the woods this afternoon, and I suspect they went further when I wasn't looking. I should have never agreed to the search party idea to begin with. It was a poor decision that we can't make again," commented Edwin.

Martha agreed by saying, "If Boomer was lost, we'd appreciate all the help we can get. But let's be honest, Edwin, we've been here for how many years now? Do you ever recall a single pet surviving the deep woods? I certainly do not. Summer and Robin have been missing for days now. We have to tell the Keller family we can no longer participate in the search."

Martha and Edwin talked it over for a few minutes more. They decided it would be Martha to deliver the bad news by means of introducing her sister, a local veterinarian.

~

Meanwhile, the Keller family was deep into a conversation led by Joey.

"Dad, calling off the search was dumb! Annie and I both heard the dogs," swore Joey.

The Keller parents had a hard time believing the story. No one else reported hearing the same noise. Mr. Keller suggested to Joey that it may have been a different animal he heard. Joey rejected the idea.

Mrs. Keller inserted her opinion. "We were making all sorts of noises; they would have heard us if they were nearby. Don't you think they would have come running over?"

Joey slammed his arm cast on the table. "I'm not making this up! Annie, tell them what you heard!"

Annie was upset but kept her cool. "Dad, mom, I'm positive I heard the dogs too. We know how their barks sound. The barking was slight, it was definitely coming from far away, but it had to be them."

"Yeah, we were probably a half mile from them, but instead of going deeper into the woods to rescue our dogs, we're sitting at a picnic table and losing daylight by the second," said Joey.

The conversation went back and forth like that for another fifteen minutes. The kids wanted to keep combing the woods, but after the poison oak cases and incoming lightning storms, the Keller parents denied their request repeatedly.

"I'm not one to give up kids," said Mrs. Keller. "But we spent the whole day out there. To ask everyone to just keep searching because you think you heard something is unreasonable. Plus, the lightning is just too dangerous."

Annie was flustered. "I don't think I heard something; I know I heard something! So did Joey, and we believe we heard Summer and Robin."

Joey scoffed. "We're wasting our time trying to convince them. They're set in their decision."

Trying not to lose his cool, Mr. Keller chimed in with a soft voice of reason, "Sometimes we think we hear things simply because we want to hear them, and it's also fair to say you are both tired. The combination of the two can lead the mind into playing tricks. Either way, I'm not going to compromise your safety. And the parents of the other campers would be very upset if we kept them out there in a lightning storm."

"Dad, please, we can grab the flashlights," begged Joey. "You need to believe me. They are out there – I heard them."

"Pal, I want to believe you, but don't forget how many lies you've told this past year," replied Mitchell.

"Come on, dad. I know back at school, I would lie about feeling sick to get out of class or lie about how many hours of video games I played. But this is different. I'm telling the truth; I *heard* them barking!"

"Joey, I know it is different, but I am telling you that no person other than your sister heard the dogs. And with all the elements being what they are, we need to regroup, case closed," said Mr. Keller.

A light rain started to fall. The Keller family gathered themselves to head inside but heard footsteps approaching. It was Martha, holding an umbrella and a cell phone. She felt uneasy interrupting the Keller family, but her face said it all. She had something important to share.

"Hi, Martha," greeted Mrs. Keller. "How is Edwin doing?"

"He's a lucky man; it could have been worse. He will be okay."

"How can we help you, Martha?" asked Mr. Keller.

She held up her phone. "I was hoping you would talk to my sister, Louisa. She's the local veterinarian. I explained your situation to her, and she wanted to share her expert opinion."

Joey asked his father to put the call on speaker. Mrs. Keller agreed, then offered his greeting. "Hello, Louisa. I am Mitchell Keller. I am here with my wife Francine and our kids Joey and Annie."

Louisa explained to the family her experience with pets lost in the woods. Apparently, lost dogs like Robin and Summer were not entirely unique.

"I've been the vet up here for ten years," explained Louisa. "I've dealt with dozens of missing animal cases when it comes to the northern woods."

"How many of those cases have happy endings?" asked Mr. Keller.

A long silence took over the call. Knowing the kids were listening made the answer all the more difficult.

Louisa answered, "None."

"So are you saying there is zero chance Robin and Summer are still alive?" asked Joey solemnly.

"I'm sorry," said Louisa. "But the chances of you finding your dogs, especially after so many days, are minuscule. The woods extend for thousands of acres. They run miles and miles deep. The terrain is harsh, and the wildlife can be even harsher. And then tack on the timing of it all. As you've seen, we get storms on most nights this late in the season. Small dogs, even the best trained, would have virtually no chance of surviving this long. I am sorry to say this to you, but I don't want to see anyone getting hurt out there."

Skeptical of the doom and gloom narrative, Annie politely issued a request, "Can you give us details on some of the situations you've dealt with?"

Louisa listed her recent cases.

"Last year, a local fisherman brought his Australian shepherd to the river. Minutes into casting his line, a bear showed up. The dog ran straight for the woods out of fear. The dog was never seen again."

She continued with another story, "Then there's my neighbor, Barbara. She lost her black cat after it chased a chipmunk into the woods. Also, never found."

Martha inserted her opinion. "It's crazier out there than you think. Louisa, tell the Kellers about Mrs. Quail."

Louisa responded, "That poor lady was out on the hiking trails training her puppy chihuahua how to walk without a leash. Out of nowhere, a massive hawk swoops in and scoops the little fella. She captured most of it on her cell phone. I saw the video myself. She eventually found the dog, but not alive."

Francine looked at Martha and said, "I wish I had known these stories earlier. I feel so bad for the animals and the owners."

Louisa responded, "I don't mean to be the bearer of bad news, but I thought I would share this information with you after Martha told me about today's search and how it came up empty."

Joey jumped in, "I guess Martha didn't tell you that we heard our dogs barking."

Mitchell had heard enough from all sides. He tried to end the call abruptly but also politely by saying a quick *thank you*.

"Before you go, allow me to add one last thing," added Louisa. "If Robin and Summer do make it out alive, I advise you get the two of them to my office *immediately*. Between ticks, bugs, poison ivy, and the wild in general, those dogs will need to be treated. Don't dwell or wait. Get them to me as fast as you can if you're given a chance – even if it is late at night, Martha will wake me up, and I will be ready to help."

The phone call ended.

Just as Martha expected, the Keller parents were spooked by Louisa's stories. Surprisingly, the call had the opposite effect on the kids. They were now more determined to continue with the search.

Martha felt obligated to provide more details surrounding the dangers of the woods and how the local animal control agency will not send out agents in the field unless it pertains to a wildlife issue. Meaning they don't assist in the search for lost pets – they don't have the human resources or budget. This agitated Annie and Joey, but it did not deter them.

"I am going back out tomorrow morning first thing," said Joey.

Martha decided to hold nothing back. "Joey, we looked all around the perimeters today. And we all ventured a little deeper than we should have. But if you go deeper, you're talking about facing bears, coyotes, wolves, snakes, bobcats, and God knows what else out there. I served in the U.S. military, and I'm scared of nothing. But I am telling you straight out that I wouldn't venture deep into those woods unless I was armed."

"So we should just leave them out there, even though we heard them bark?" asked Annie with a bit of an attitude.

"I understand your pain, Annie. But you have to understand our dilemma. The liability for us is too great. I cannot put the campers or our staff in harm's way, so we can longer participate in the search. I hope you understand our position," said Martha.

"We certainly do," responded Mitchell. "And we thank you for all that's been done."

Martha chimed in with one last thought. "I do offer one bit of hope. Those northern woods end at the mountain; the strongest of dogs would never get up and over the mountain. So, if they are still out there, if they are still alive after all this time, then it means they've been roaming around in circles. Perhaps there is a chance they will find their way out of the woods considering there isn't any place else left to go."

It wasn't the most endearing message of hope, but it helped reassure Joey and Annie that they did hear those barks and that their dogs were still alive. Summer and Robin had to be the exception. Their story of survival would be an anomaly! It would be the story Louisa would share someday in the future with another distraught family instead of the horrifying stories she shared with the Kellers.

Chapter 22
The Pack

The thunder and lightning had stopped. Night three officially started. It was the first night with no rain since the dogs had been lost. A full moon served as a source of light, illuminating the forest. For some reason, it was spookier than the stormy nights. Without the rain, Robin could hear all the different sounds and noises that came about in the evening hours.

It had been a few hours since Robin left Summer's side. During that time, Robin struggled with the guilt of leaving his sister behind. In addition, the pain and numbness from the snake bite became more intense, spreading to his back.

Out of nowhere, Robin heard a faint-sounding howl at his back. It came from the direction where he had left Summer, or so he thought. Robin stood still, waiting for the chance to hear it again. A minute passed, and he heard nothing. He slowly marched forward a few steps, but Robin stopped again – his instincts told him to wait.

Robin nervously stood in place for a few seconds more, wishing the sound would repeat itself, but it did not. Even so, he decided to retreat back to Summer.

But Robin lost the trail. He attempted to retrace his footsteps but could not find the route leading back to his sister. Robin wanted nothing more than to be with Summer. Leaving her was a dumb idea. He should have waited it out with her, no matter the outcome. He would rather succumb to the woods with his sister than be alone. If he never saw Summer again, he would be unable to continue living, knowing that he had failed her.

An hour went by searching, then another. The scenery felt the same; he thought he was going in circles. Nothing carried a scent of familiarity.

Ugly thoughts and horrible questions crept into his mind.

What kind of animal made the howl he believed to have heard earlier? Whatever it is, Summer can't defend herself.

Did the fox find her? It would kill her if he had.

Do snakes come out at night? She can't run away if they do.

Knowing Summer was alone, injured, and defenseless, Robin picked up his pace. He struggled to ignore his pains and tried to place all of his focus on finding a path back to her.

What made the search even more excruciating was resisting the urge to bark. At night, predators of all kinds are out and about. Robin could not risk drawing their attention.

A spooky ground fog blanketed the forest. The moon's glow was so bright that Robin felt exposed. But everything was perfectly still and quiet. The northern woods felt utterly abandoned.

Aaaauuuuuhhhhhhh.

Robin heard a resounding cry echo through the forest. A dying, bellowing cry. A cry from pain and suffering. It sounded dreadful.

Aaaauuuuhhhhhhh. Aaaauuuuuhhhhhhh.

Robin cautiously followed the sounds of the cries, which sounded more like moans of agony. Whatever was making this noise sounded physically hurt. And it was something big, meaning it was definitely not Summer.

Aaaauuuuuhhhhhhh.

Over the edge of a large dirt mound was an oval-ringed divot in the forest. It was covered chiefly by stone pebbles and aging moss. The edges were a mesh of sod and rock. The divot appeared to be an old pond that had dried out over time. It was also the source of the agonizing bellows.

Robin peered over from the dirt mound, seeing an injured creature about twenty feet away. It was a massive male deer.

The buck was a magnificent creature, but one of his hind legs was snapped in the shape of a *V.* Robin could see bones protruding from his knee where the break had happened. The buck couldn't move. He could only wail in pain.

Robin wondered what had happened to him. Maybe the deer had fallen into this barren pond, breaking his leg. Was he running towards something? Or away from something?

Aaaauuuuuhhhhhhh.

Aaaah-wooooooo.

The deer's cry was returned with a howl. The howl sounded closer to the one he had heard earlier. Then a series of groans rang out. Suddenly, Robin remembered the howling sounds from the night before in the bear den. He and Summer had also heard the same howls during the summer RV trip. The Keller parents ushered the kids into the camper every time there was howling.

These were the howls of wolves.

A pack of four descended into the divot, on the opposite side of where Robin was hiding. They could not see Robin past the dirt mound. Nor did they care. Their eyes were on the wounded buck. They circled the injured giant like vultures.

The buck swung its antlers wildly at the wolves. He nabbed one in the face, but another jumped on him from the other side. Then another wolf jumped on his hind leg. Soon, all four of the wolves were attacking the deer, tearing into its hide. They chewed, clawed, and scratched. The buck was defenseless. He let out more cries before slumping into an unmoving silence.

The pack of wolves showed no mercy. The buck had become a midnight meal for the ferocious wolves in a few minutes. One of them alone would struggle to take on a buck of that size, but a pack of four was unstoppable.

They let out howling shrieks into the night sky as they consumed the buck. Robin was paralyzed with fear. He had to get out of there before he was spotted. Or before they located Summer.

Robin slowly retreated his steps. But not slowly enough. His hind paw hit the dirt pile, sending pebbles down into the divot.

A wolf was alerted, the one struck by the buck's

antler. One of his eyes was bloodied and blind, but his snout worked fine. And so did his ears. He heard something *and* smelled a new presence. Robin quickly scurried away from the divot but could hear the wolf climbing up from the other side. He had to hide; fast.

The wolf mounted over the dirt pile and started sniffing for the spy. The rest of his pack paused on their deer meal, taking an interest in the search. They formed together and spread out in four separate directions, tracking the grounds for their next prey.

Thankfully, Robin burrowed deep into a small opening under a willow tree. It was an empty otter nest fortified with chewed-up logs and twigs.

Robin peered above the forest behind the miniature fortress of wood, remaining still as a statue. One slight movement could mean his end was inevitable. The wolves would tear Robin apart like a rag doll. Fear coursed through Robin's veins like ice water.

The bloodied-eyed wolf stalked close to the nest, deer blood dripping from his mouth. He ravishingly searched and sniffed for Robin. He could smell the dog but could not see him. His snout loomed over the otter nest. A grin of teeth glistened in the moonlight; the wolf bit into the wood, sensing something was living and breathing below.

One of the other wolves howled. The rest of the pack howled too. They were running back to the buck carcass. A rival pack of wolves was attempting to snag the remains of the kill. A barking and snarling battle broke out between the two groups.

The bloodied-eyed wolf abandoned his investigation of the otter nest. He returned to the divot to guard its deer meal, all but forgetting about Robin. Sensing a window of opportunity, Robin left the nest and ran far in the opposite direction of the wolves. His pain from the snake bite continued to escalate, but he could not slow down. He needed to find Summer.

Robin turned his run into a sprint, dashing through the dark forest. He pumped through spider webs and hordes of hovering mosquitoes. None of it mattered. He just had to keep searching, no matter how long it took him. Without hesitation or caution, Robin barked. Two short yet loud barks.

He waited. But he heard nothing for minutes. Depression started to sink in. He barked again. Still nothing. But he kept trying again and again.

And then he finally heard his sister's bark. And then another bark. The sound was traveling from the east. Robin followed the trajectory of the bark. He then barked again. Another bark was returned. He also heard something faint, but he was too focused on Summer's barking.

He stopped. The beautiful trees in this area were recognizable. He searched through a few more trees. And then he saw Summer lying at the base of the oak tree where he had left her. She looked sad and confused but also happy at her brother's return.

She also wasn't alone. Resting above on the branch of the oak tree was the source of the second sound: their protector and guide, the owl. Robin was happy to see him, but there was a frightened look in the owl's big, yellow eyes.

Chapter 23

One Last Try

Robin lies on his back. Tears from his eyes. Summer is on her belly, not moving. Everything around them is pitch black. Robin starts crying.

Joey runs to them, but as he gets closer, they're farther away. They cry more.

"I'm coming for you, buddy! Hang on!"

He got closer within reach, but they were disappearing again.

"No."

First Summer. Then Robin.

"No, wait!"

They were gone.

Joey woke up in a craze. He accidentally knocked over the cowbell on his dresser. He was dripping in sweat. Another nightmare, only this one was on the brink of reality. He checked his wristwatch: it was a few minutes before five o'clock in the morning.

Annie stirred awake in the cot across from him in the guest cabin. "You okay? Another nightmare?"

Joey nodded with shame. He picked up the noisy cowbell Austin had left for him. "I hope I didn't wake up mom and dad."

"I doubt it," assured Annie. "They've been exhausted. I can still hear dad snoring in the next room."

Joey gathered his cool, eyeing the cowbell. "It was a bad dream about the dogs. We shouldn't have stopped looking."

Annie stood up out of her bed. "I agree."

She went to her dresser and pulled out the whistle she used in the search yesterday. Then she started putting her jacket and boots on. Sunlight would be visible in thirty minutes, but she did not want to wait. She could not sleep all night; she only thought about Summer and Robin.

Joey followed her lead, careful not to wake up their parents. Sneaking out would get them in trouble, but they needed to be rebellious at this point. There was no time to waste.

In under a minute, Joey was dressed and ready. He also held the cowbell. "Let's give it one last try."

Annie grabbed a pen and paper to write a note to their parents: *'Joey and I went to the woods. Meet us out there.'*

Quietly, the two Keller kids left the guest cabin and ventured into the early phases of dawn. The sky was a dark blue, transitioning to light pink. It would be an hour or so before the temperature would heat up. For now, they dealt with a brisk morning chill. They hoped the dogs weren't cold wherever they were.

"Let's start where we left off on the hiking trails," suggested Annie. "Then make our way across and back around into camp."

"Good idea," said Joey. He looked at his sister with respect and admiration. "Hey, Annie?"

She turned and faced her brother.

"I hope I'm as cool and confident as you someday. I wouldn't be able to do a lot on my own. I'm thankful you're always there for me."

Annie smiled at her brother. "And I hope I'm as smart and witty as you one day. I'll always be there for you, Joey; that's what brothers and sisters are for."

The siblings high-fived one another. Their bond remained strong even when they were brutally mad at each other. A twin bond, as their dad would deem it. A genuinely unbreakable friendship.

The Keller kids continued forth into the woods. The hiking trails were a reasonable distance from the cabin, but the sounds of the cowbell and the whistle would surely wake up the other campers. And the Keller parents. But Joey and Annie knew these noise-makers were their best bet with the dogs. They had to try.

They started ringing and whistling all throughout the forest. Birds took to the sky, hares dashed away into bushes, and deer sped in retreat. The sounds filled the morning void.

Ring, whistle, ring, whistle...

~

Mr. Keller and Mrs. Keller were deep asleep. They were exhausted and beat from the past few days, so much so that they slept through the sounds of their children readying themselves to explore the woods.

Dawn had only just bloomed when Mr. Keller's

alarm clock rang. He rose from his bed to make a cup of coffee in the kitchen when he found Annie's note.

Mr. Keller yelled into his bedroom. "Francine, the kids left the cabin to look for the dogs without us."

"Gotta give them credit for trying," remarked Mrs. Keller, who was now awake.

Mr. Keller opened the door and could hear the cowbell in the distance.

Mrs. Keller heard the sounds too. "You should call for them to come inside before they wake up the rest of the camp. We need to start packing, as much as I hate to admit it."

"They won't be happy to hear that," said Mr. Keller.

Before he left the cabin, his coffee routine was interrupted by his cell phone ringing. It was dreadfully loud.

The Caller ID on his phone read *Felix*. They exchanged numbers after they finished searching the woods the other day. He said he would call if he learned anything new or had any updates.

Mr. Keller quickly answered. "Felix?"

"Good morning, Mitchell," said Felix with elation. "Sorry to call so early."

Verona was heard in the background, saying hello to the Kellers. Mr. Keller hit the speaker button so his wife could listen to the conversation.

"What can I do for you, Felix?"

"Any luck finding your dogs yet?"

Mr. Keller sighed. "Unfortunately, no. We searched the woods next to Wilderness World yesterday. No sign of them, though my kids believe they heard them barking a long distance away."

"Do you think they really heard them?"

"I'm not sure, to be honest. There were many of us out there, yet only Annie and Joey heard them. I want to believe it was the dogs, but odds are it's wishful thinking."

"Well, I'm calling to offer an opportunity. My old friend Jacques-Pierre – *we call him JP* – is in town at his cabin. Anyways, he came over last night to visit Verona and me. I told him the story about your dogs lost in the woods. He offered to help in a big way."

"How so?" asked Mrs. Keller, joining in on the conversation.

"JP is a pilot. And he has his helicopter here. He offered to take you folks flying and give you the ultimate bird's eye view. He believes you'll find the dogs better that way. He can cover the areas between Wilderness World and the interstate gas station."

Mr. Keller and Mrs. Keller exchanged thoughtful glances. Could this be the solution?

"That's a generous offer, Felix," said Mr. Keller. "How much would that cost?"

"Well, JP is a friend of mine and can give you a discounted price of $1,500 for the day. So you're basically covering the fuel cost."

Mr. Keller gulped. His wife felt uneasy too. It was a lot of money. He felt reluctant to spend that kind of money, considering finances were tight.

Mrs. Keller felt the same way. How beneficial would this ride be?

"How many of us can you bring on the helicopter?"

"It's a four-seater, so just two of you. I'll be going to help navigate. That leaves two seats in the back. I'm assuming you're taking one of them, Mitch?"

The other part of this offer that made Mr. Keller uneasy was the idea of flying in the helicopter. He has only been on a few planes, but he had a general fear of flying. And anything to do with heights. But at the end of the day, he was willing to volunteer if it meant helping find the dogs.

"We want to take you up on the offer," announced Mrs. Keller unexpectedly. "And I would like a seat on the helicopter."

Mr. Keller turned to her in surprise. "Actually, Felix, can you give us a minute?"

"Sure thing, but decide soon. JP can only fly it today. It's supposed to get windy tonight and then stormy again for the rest of the week. It would be today or nothing."

"Gotcha. Give me a few minutes, and I'll put you on hold."

Mr. Keller muted the phone and turned to his wife. "No way. We can't spend that money, and I'm not comfortable with you going on some stranger's helicopter without me."

"We have no choice. As tight as our budget is, we have the money to do this. It could be our only chance. And you *hate* flying. The point of this ride is to be alert and vigilant. That'll be hard for you to do if you can't look out the window without almost vomiting."

"The money you speak of is put away for Annie and Joey's college; I don't want to deplete that fund," said Mitchell.

"Really, Mitch, are you kidding? Ask your son and daughter if they mind taking a part of their college fund to find the dogs. You know what they'll say."

Mitchell knew his wife was correct.

"Okay fine, I won't argue that. But I'm not a big fan of the idea though. Who is taking the other open seat?" questioned Mitchell.

Mrs. Keller thought about it for a moment. "Annie will. I don't think it's a good idea if Joey goes with his wrist broken."

"Not loving the idea of my wife and daughter going up hundreds of feet into the air at the cost of fifteen hundred dollars," replied Mr. Keller. "Especially without me there."

Fran looked at him with a side-eye. "It's not about the money. If the kids knew there was a chance like this to find the dogs, they would be begging you to take it. And if they knew you rejected the opportunity, they'd be furious."

He sighed because he knew she was right. The kids would *beg* to use the helicopter if it meant finding Robin and Summer.

Mr. Keller nodded. "Let's do it."

He unmuted his phone. "We'll do it, Felix. Francine and my daughter Annie will be the passengers."

"Great! I'll let JP know. We'll pick you up in an hour," instructed Felix.

Mr. Keller went outside. He was surprised to see Martha up and about. The large, no-nonsense woman was carrying freshly cut wood logs to a large fire pit. Boomer was outside following her routine before residing on the main house porch.

"Good morning Martha," said Mr. Keller.

"Good morning. The ringing and whistling I hear in the woods, is that Joey and Annie?"

"Yes, it is. They're determined not to give up."

"Well, I figured starting a fire would help to send up a smoke signal for the dogs," said Martha. "Chances are low they'll see or smell it, but it could be worth a shot."

Mr. Keller acknowledged the gesture. Martha went into the main cabin house to start breakfast. Meanwhile, Mr. Keller walked over to his children, who were trekking toward the garden area. They saw their father approaching.

"We're sorry," offered Annie modestly.

"Don't be; I totally understand," said Mr. Keller. "Martha is making breakfast. Let's go eat with your mother; there's something we have to talk about."

"Can we search one more time after breakfast?" asked Joey.

"You and I will, but there's something your sister and mother will be doing instead," answered Mr. Keller. "First, let's eat. Then we'll discuss."

"But if we stop now, we may miss them," pushed back Annie. "Every minute counts."

"You guys need food in your stomachs before we continue on. Like I said, your mom and I need to talk to you guys first before we go back to searching."

Joey and Annie both sighed, though they were curious. They had been searching for an hour. Tiredness and lack of sleep began to creep in on them. Too fatigued to protest further, the siblings followed their dad's lead, abandoning the cowbell and whistle.

By the time they reached the main house cabin, they were out of range to hear a noise that would have changed everything.

Chapter 24
Pitch Black

Dawn crept from the east, but the dogs hadn't slept. It was their third morning waking up in the woods, day four in total. The owl hovered above them, nestled in a tree and remaining alert. It was as if he had encountered something that spooked him.

For Robin, he thought about the wolves tearing into the deer carcass. The horrifying image burned into his head. He then thought about his snake bite. The pain was becoming unbearable. It looked infected.

Summer was not faring well either. The pain in her hind leg made every movement unbearable. They wouldn't make it another day in the woods. But they were going to try at least once more to find a way out rather than succumb to the woods.

A heavy morning fog crept into the forest. Visibility was limited to a mere few feet at best. This meant they were exposed to whatever could be lurking out there. And something was always lurking.

Then they heard the ringing. And the whistling.

And then they heard their names shouted.

"Robin! Summer!"

It sounded just like Annie and Joey. It was impossible to tell where the shouts and noises were coming from. They sounded distant, almost totally out of range, like a fading echo. Robin questioned if he was hallucinating from the snake bite.

Excitement took hold of them as they heard more ringing, more whistling. The fog made it impossible to pin-point any discernible direction. Visibility was cloudy, yet the dogs could hear the calls for their names. They limped in what they believed was the direction of the voices. The owl trailed them.

The ringing sounded a bit closer. The noise was now accompanied by Joey and Annie yelling their names again. Both dogs barked in concert with the ringing, two times each.

The dogs stopped walking. They wanted to be sure of the direction. Summer and Robin listened for the next set of rings, but the ringing stopped.

They waited a few minutes in place. No ringing. Robin gave off a bark, but still no ringing. Summer barked repeatedly. But no ringing.

Ten minutes passed. Then twenty minutes passed. No voices. No ringing. No whistles. Whatever the dogs had heard, they lost it. This devastated the last morsels of hope within them.

The early morning sunlight was working its way up, brightening the forest and clearing some fog as the winds picked up.

Oddly, the owl disappeared after the noises stopped. He flew high into the air, out of sight of the dogs. It appeared he was going after something. And now, Robin and Summer were alone again.

Another hour passed. All they could see within their surroundings were trees, dirt, grass, more trees, fallen logs, and more and more trees. It felt like an endless time loop of green and brown. A forest that refused to let them leave.

Their minds started to wander about Joey and Annie. For Summer, she thought of snuggling close to the children on warm summer nights and frigid winter evenings. In Robin's mind, memories of the countless hours of fetch in the backyard were complimented by head and tummy scratches out of pure love.

Robin and Summer longed for this affection. They wanted it more than anything in the world, except for maybe food and fresh water. Hunger and dehydration continued to set in. Without the Kellers, their lives would never be the same. Something deep within the dogs told them that Joey and Annie were ringing and whistling.

They wondered if the Kellers would move on and adopt different dogs. The idea alone broke their hearts, but something deep within Robin and Summer told them the Keller kids would never give up looking for them.

The daydreaming was cut short by the return of the owl. He looked panicked; he had come from the south, which was the opposite direction of where they had been traveling. It seemed as if the owl had seen a ghost. Or something worse.

Then Robin picked up on a scent. Summer too. They looked at each other, recognizing the scent's familiarity. And hostility. They then heard the movement of something breaking through a bush. The owl turned his head to the bush, as did both dogs.

About thirty feet away, skulking through a flower bush, was the fox. His bright, ginger-red fur stood out in the backdrop of greenery. The fox stared directly at the dogs, licking its lips and snout. He had been searching for them ever since the river encounter.

This was it, the dogs thought. The journey would end as a meal served fresh to a ferocious fox.

Not without a chase, at least. Robin and Summer, despite their injuries, leapt into a sprint. They did not look back, but they winced in pain with every forward moment. And they could hear the fox jump into pursuit. The owl swooped down to claw the fox, but the crimson predator held him off. The owl was powerless in this pursuit. He could only hope for the best.

The chase ensued through the forest. For every few feet traveled, the fox closed more distance. Soon he was only about fifteen feet behind the dogs. During the chase, they passed by the skeletal remains of the deer from last night. The smell of decay almost threw the dogs off balance. It briefly drew the fox's attention as well.

Summer dove into a bush, as did Robin. The fox attempted to leap in after them, but one of the branches ricocheted back into the fox's face, stunning him momentarily.

Taking advantage of the incapacitated fox, the dogs cut through a few more bushes, attempting to throw off the pursuit. But, as the fog cleared and the winds picked up, they realized they would no longer have a natural cover. They needed somewhere efficient to hide.

The owl flew forward in front of the dogs, leading them to a destination. They probably only had a few seconds before the fox would catch up again. Following the owl diligently, they discovered their next hideout.

A cave. It was a large, circular pitch black entrance into the base of the mountain they had used as their focal point. Way larger than a bear's den but also much creepier and ominous.

But Robin and Summer had no choice. This was their best solution if they wanted to hide from the fox. They scurried into the cave, surrounded in complete darkness. It was cold, rocky, and damp inside. No sunlight breached the interior of the cave, only the outer entrance. It was the perfect cover.

The owl remained outside the cave, perched on a close by tree at the base of the mountain. It was scoping for the whereabouts of the fox.

As they traveled farther into the cave, the dogs heard an echoing, shrieking noise coming deep from within.

Chapter 25

Eye in the Sky

"How old is that thing, mom?"

Annie looked on in disbelief as she walked towards the aging helicopter. Discolored and rusty in spots, Annie had never seen anything like it before.

"Do all helicopters look like this?" Annie asked her mother.

"Shhhhh," responded her mother. "Don't be rude."

Annie was nervous, to begin with, and now seeing the helicopter's aging condition made the fear even greater.

Sensing her daughter's concern, Francine emphasized the benefits of a bird's eye view. "If the dogs are out there, then this is the best opportunity we can ask for."

The airfield was near Wilderness World, located closer to the mountainside. Annie had seen it during the initial drive up to camp earlier in the summer. Now she and her mother were walking across the tarmac with Felix.

"Don't let the look of this chopper scare you; it's no different than the rust spots on your dad's minivan," said Felix.

"I'm fine," said Annie. "I'll do anything to find the dogs. I know I heard them; I know they're out there."

Felix gave Francine and Annie a thumbs up as the helicopter blades began to spin. The noise of the blades was blaring, and the wind they gave off was super powerful.

Annie's hair was blowing in a million directions. Her

mother's hair was tucked under a baseball cap, but it was barely staying on her head. Both ladies looked to Felix for guidance.

"JP is in the chopper, ready to go, and I'm sorry for the rushed introduction, but you'll meet him as you buckle in," shouted Felix. "We have limited time before the weather turns on us. We've gotta get up now."

Mrs. Keller turned to Annie and shouted, "Are you comfortable doing this?"

Annie nodded modestly.

Felix escorted them to the helicopter as it prepared for takeoff. They were brought inside the cabin and given headsets to communicate. JP, an older gentleman with a scraggly white beard and a silver ponytail, gave them a salute.

"Welcome aboard, ladies!"

JP had a charming smile and a sense of worldly adventurism. But his outfit was less than what Annie expected from a seasoned pilot. His Grateful Dead t-shirt looked older than he did, and his blue jeans were worn and unwashed.

"I'll go over a few rules, and then we shall take off," said JP. "But most importantly, I want you to know I love dogs; here's my Goldendoodle puppy."

He took out a polaroid picture from his wallet. It was a photo of his wife at a swimming pool, caressing the fluffiest poodle Annie had ever seen. It made her yearn for the presence of Summer.

"His name is Jerry; we named him after the greatest

musician of all time – Jerry Garcia," explained JP. "I think I'd cry myself a river if I lost him in the woods."

JP went over the safety rules quickly with them. He mentioned the high winds that would kick in at some point in the afternoon. They were going to have to be speedy in their journey. The plan was to cover as much area as possible without risking safety. All in, JP estimated it would be two hours.

"I have a check for you. I just need to know to whom I should make it payable," said Francine.

"We'll worry about money at the end of the ride. For now, just strap in, and enjoy my music." JP jubilantly announced as he popped in a cassette. Playing in the headsets was the song *Dark Star.*

JP began singing along with Jerry Garcia and the Grateful Dead, *"Dark Star crashes, pouring its light into ashes. Reason tatters, the forces tear loose from the axis."*

Annie and Francine looked at each other with slight concern. And then presto! The chopper was airborne as a guitar rifted in their ears.

Annie's eyes widened with astonishment, and her belly tickled from the sudden lift. She looked out her side window. The ground beneath her was growing more distant by the second. She looked at her mother and chuckled with uncertainty. Francine smiled in return, and she grabbed Annie's hand to provide reassurance that everything was going to be fine.

The helicopter was soaring high into the air in a matter of minutes. She could see the vastness of tall forest trees, folding into one another like one large pallet of evergreen. Toward the west were the mountains commonly used for hiking and outdoor camping.

They reached higher altitudes by the minute. Across the horizon was nothing but blue sky. It was late morning, heading into noon. It was the perfect time to observe everything below.

JP looked at Felix. "I love this version of the song. It's twenty-three minutes, man. No better song ever made."

Felix smiled.

JP turned his attention to the girls. "Ladies, take a look out the port side!"

"He means to your left," clarified Felix.

They peered down below, spotting Wilderness World.

~

They all stepped out of the main cabin house to view the approaching helicopter. Joey stood in the gravel driveway, waving as best he could with his cast, hoping his sister and mother would see him. Then all the campers waved, including Martha. Boomer yelped at the sound of the helicopter hovering above. They watched the helicopter pass through the camp until it was out of sight, heading south.

"Makes my stomach queasy just seeing them up that high," commented Mr. Keller. "I'm sorry we couldn't go up with them, pal."

Joey shrugged. "I don't care who finds the dogs, and

I don't care how it's done. So can we do something too, dad?"

Mr. Keller responded, "Want to go back to the woods with the cowbell?"

Joey smiled. "Definitely."

Joey informed the other campers that he and his dad would search in the woods. Austin, Oliver, Kirsten, Emily, and everyone else wanted to help but had to follow Edwin and Martha's rules. So the Keller father and son duo made their way to the forest.

He turned to his father. "I want to apologize for my behavior the last few days. Actually, the last few weeks. Maybe even months? I've said nasty things about you and mom, and I've been spoiled. I know that a helicopter ride costs a lot of money, and I appreciate how hard you work for our family."

Mr. Keller smiled. "It's funny, you and your sister truly have twin telepathy – she apologized to me right before she left for the airfield with your mother."

Mitch then kneeled down to face his son. "Joey, your apology is accepted, and I want you to know that being your dad is the greatest privilege of my entire life. And don't worry about the money; the value of family is priceless. Summer and Robin are our family, and I can't think of a single thing I'd rather spend money on than finding those dogs."

"Not even front-row tickets to the Superbowl?" joked Joey.

"Nope, not even if I was the starting quarterback," Mr. Keller answered with a smile. "Seriously, I owe you an apology too. I'm sorry the last few months have been filled with me talking about money and the store, and I've been overly tough on everyone. It's been constant stress, and I've failed by negatively impacting everyone – even Robin and Summer."

Joey shook his head. "You didn't fail. You're the best dad in the world. You're also my hero. I want to be just like you when I grow up. Nobody is as great as you."

Mr. Keller joked, "Not even Batman?"

"Hmmm. Can I have a minute to think about that one?" answered Joey.

They both laughed.

Seeing Joey happy drove a genuine warmness through Mitchel's heart. He couldn't resist and hugged his son. Finally, the tensions that had built up for so long started to settle and ease. It was therapeutic.

Joey then proposed an idea. "Maybe once we're back home, I can help you at the store since Harold is gone."

"Not a bad idea; maybe I'll make you a partner one day," quipped Mitch.

Chapter 26
What Flies in Darkness

The unnerving eeriness of the dark cave crept on Robin and Summer as they realized they were surrounded by bats.

Hundreds of silvery, glowing eyes stared down upon them from the spiked ceiling of the cave. Shriveling shrieks emerged from above for minutes. Then silence.

A smell overwhelmed Robin and Summer. Bat poop. It was everywhere on the floor, inside crevices and cracks, and painted on the rocks and walls of the cave. It was falling from above too.

The bats were alarmed by the sudden arrival of Robin and Summer but remained stationed deep within the cave, where they hung upside down in uninterrupted dormancy.

The dogs crept behind a jagged rock. They did not like the presence of the bats or their poop. But bats were nothing new to them. Throughout the past two summers at the Keller house, bats would take off into the night, shrilling between one another. The shrill noises irritated Robin and Summer, prompting them to bark into the sky.

Robin saw bats in the Batman comic books Joey read. Even so, the ones lingering in the cave were more terrifying than the ones in the comics or the ones that flew through their backyard.

The bats were the least of their problems. They were more concerned about the whereabouts of the fox. Hours had gone by since Robin and Summer escaped his pursuit. They felt confident they had lost him, but there was still an uneasiness about leaving the cave. Plus, the chase exasperated them. Robin's snake bite grew worse, and Summer's throbbing hind leg felt ready to fall off her body. All in, the dogs knew the cave provided them a hiding spot, and much-needed rest, despite the lurking bats hanging above them. Robin closed his eyes and began to snore. Summer followed his lead.

An hour passed.

The dogs slowly woke from their naps, realizing they were still trapped in the cave. Hope persisted that they efficiently lost the fox. But did that mean they also lost their owl friend? Did the fox hunt him? Where did he go?

Their solitude was interrupted by a noise that sounded like the air was being chopped inside a blender. It was not the fox nor the owl. It was much bigger, and it sounded unnatural. The noise was mechanical and motorized, coming from the sky outside.

It was the sound of a helicopter. That was something the dogs had familiarity with, too, though seldomly. Back at the Keller house, there were days during the year when a helicopter would pass overhead while Robin and Summer played in the backyard. The surprising yet jarring sound from the sky machines always startled the dogs in their tracks. It always came without warning.

Instinct told the dogs to run out of the cave and investigate the sounds of the helicopter. But the risk was too high. If the fox was lurking just outside the entrance of the cave, Robin and Summer would have no means of escape.

In the cave, they had the element of surprise. Total blackness, hidden from plain view. The dogs would have the upper hand over the fox if he entered. And the bats would likely despise his presence.

The approaching noise of the helicopter hit a crescendo and then started to fade away distantly. Wherever it was going, it was heading out from the mountain. Any chance to see the chopper, or to be seen by it, was gone.

Robin and Summer had no time to dwell on if they made a mistake because now they were faced with their re-curring problem.

A sound of paw prints scratching leaf debris erupted through the silence. The scent of danger filled the nostrils of the dogs. They did not have to peer over their hiding rock to know the fox had arrived.

The fox was at the cave entrance, slowly walking into the darkness at a snail's pace. As he investigated the shadowy chamber, short, stuttering sniffs came from his snout. He had no idea the dogs were hiding about ten feet away to the left side of the cave. But soon, he would.

The dogs needed to act fast. They questioned how they would slip by him undetected. It felt impossible.

A memory came to Robin about Joey. One night, they were lying in his bed while watching an old Batman cartoon. In one of the scenes, Batman used a loud sonar device to draw out swarms of bats. Maybe that's something the dogs would have to do but with barking. Bats prefer to be in darkness during daylight hours, but they'll leave the cave if spooked, regardless of the time of day.

While debating their next move, the dogs heard something else from outside the cave. Hooting.

The owl had returned. He blasted out a loud hoot. The fox was not happy about the owl's presence. The red-coated predator let out a low, rumbling growl.

Robin took charge. He knew there was no time to waste. It was risky, but he barked loudly. Summer followed his lead. A choral of barks echoed throughout the cave. They exposed their position to the fox.

But before the fox could react, a legion of dark, fuzzy vampire bats flew from the cave's ceiling to its entrance.

Robin and Summer's plan half-worked. The bats swarmed and swallowed the fox into a dizzy darkness; he was almost immobilized. They scratched up his face and body, and he had no source of protection. But the act only made him angrier. He chomped back at the bats, killing and desecrating about three.

There was no clear opening for the dogs to sneak by the fox. Instead, he blatantly stood in the middle of the entrance, unmoving despite the swarm. He *knew* the dogs were in there.

All of the bats exited the cave. It was daytime, but the nocturnal creatures flew high in the sun. This left the fox free of distraction and blindness. Robin and Summer had one choice of direction: head deeper into the cave.

~

189

The Grateful Dead song had ended, but JP didn't dare concern himself with changing cassettes. He was too focused on controlling the helicopter as the winds pushed it hard to the left. Then hard to the right. Then left again.

The high winds had kicked in faster than JP anticipated. Piloting the helicopter to remain steady was proving daunting. His passengers could feel it too.

"Sorry about this, folks; we're experiencing more turbulence than expected."

Annie squeezed her mother's hand tight. The inconsistent balance made her feel somewhat sick to her stomach. She looked to her mother for support. Francine gave a motherly smile. The kind that makes a child feel that all is okay. But the truth was Francine feared for their safety. Even so, keeping Annie strong and focused was her only job.

"Keep looking for the dogs," instructed Francine.

The helicopter bounced up and down. Annie gripped her mother's hand as she looked for any sign, any clue to the whereabouts of Summer and Robin.

"I'm going to take us lower," said JP. "You'll see the river on the port side. If I was a dog, that's where I would be."

Annie recognized the spot; they had encountered it the other day. She pressed her forehead against the glass window. But as sharp-eyed as Annie was, she saw nothing. No explicit, distinct piece of evidence of the dogs' existence. It worried her, which her mother was able to detect.

"Hang in there, honey," said Mrs. Keller into her headset.

Annie smiled. But her smile disappeared in a nanosecond after the helicopter was blasted with a strong wind from the west. The helicopter shifted course as a result.

Francine's fake smile was gone. She was now biting her lip. Annie knew it was her turn to provide distraction. She wanted to say a lot to her mother, and now was the time to say it.

"I'm sorry about how my behavior has been, mom. And for breaking the promise to you and dad. I apologized to him earlier, but I wanted to tell you too. You mean the world to me, and I know Joey feels the same way."

Suddenly, Mrs. Keller forgot about the chopper's turbulent ride. She smiled from ear to ear and then kissed her daughter's hand. "You're a real all-star, Annie Keller. I love you and your brother more than you'll ever know."

The loving moment was broken by heavy turbulence that shook the cabin. Then a crackle sounded on their headsets. It was JP. "Hate to interrupt, but I wanted to inform you we have to head back towards the airport; we have to abandon the search."

"These winds are brutal," added Felix. "The storm is approaching faster than expected from the south. You can see the clouds forming in the distance."

Annie and her mother looked out the port side window. They could see dark gray clouds forming with a purple underbelly. Small little cusps of lightning were flashing in violet streaks within the clouds. It felt ominous.

JP began circling the chopper into a one-hundred-eighty-degree turn, heading back north. The winds made the turn shaky. Annie gripped her mother's hand tighter. Francine looked at Felix. For the first time during the ride, he appeared nervous too.

The wind continued to batter the helicopter. JP tried bringing it to a lower altitude to stifle the shakiness. As he hovered above the tree line, passing over the river again, his jaw dropped.

"What the heck?"

They all looked to the north as JP pointed to the mountain. They all saw it. A plume of fluttery darkness against the north's clear blue sky. If the storm was ominous, this appeared more apocalyptic.

"Are those birds?" asked Annie. "Migrating geese, perhaps?"

The flying mass flew in their direction. Thousands upon thousands of birds soaring high and in spirals. Their origin was from the base of the mountain.

"Those are bats, not birds," confirmed JP.

"Why are bats flying during the day?" asked Francine. "Aren't they nocturnal?"

Felix answered, "Yes, they sleep in caves during the day. Something must have spooked them."

Felix's statement sifted in Annie's mind. *What could have spooked them?*

Before she could calculate the possibilities, an off-shooting swarm of bats flew directly into the helicopter's path, enveloping the aircraft.

"Holy cow, this is a first!" yelled JP into the headset. The bats blocked any visibility in the windshield and the windows on the chopper's sides. Annie was both marveled and horrified. Francine felt the same way. It was incredible, but it felt threatening.

JP struggled to correctly navigate the helicopter between the bats and the winds. "I'm going to drop us down more; hang on!"

Annie and her mother felt a lurch in their stomachs as the helicopter descended fast. It felt like a roller coaster but with less guidance. There were no tracks. They were practically free-falling. They shut their eyes tight.

Felix was uneasy. "JP, we should get back to the airfield!"

"It's hard to see anything right now, Felix; I'm trying."

The helicopter dovetailed to the left, attempting to shake itself off the bats' path. Annie bumped into her mother as they slid and descended more. She yelled with fright.

"Mom, I'm scared!"

"Hang on, Annie, it's going to be okay!" replied Francine. She continued, "Felix, what is happening?"

He didn't answer. Instead, he looked at JP with alarming concern as the aging pilot tried to control the rusted rudder.

"Come on, damn it!" JP said with frustration.

Moments of struggle ensued, but eventually, JP straightened out the chopper. They were flying just barely above the trees now. It was getting dangerously close.

Annie called out from the back seat, "Please don't crash, JP."

A tear ran down Francine's face. All she could do was hold her daughter's hand and think about her family. She thought about how much she loved Joey, Annie, Mitchell, Robin, and Summer. She silently begged God to give her more time. She pleaded for another chance for her family to be all together. She wanted one more moment, a time to repeatedly share her feelings out loud to all of them: "I love you, I love you, I love you."

Felix looked back at Fran and Annie; he saw their fear. He bowed his head in defeat. There was nothing more he could do. He felt guilty about convincing the Keller ladies to come in the helicopter.

JP pulled on the controls to elevate higher, avoiding all possibility of collision.

Annie felt herself gravitating now. She closed her eyes and imagined Joey's state as if he were subjected to this nightmarish ride. Then she thought about the first time she and her brother held Robin and Summer. It made her smile.

As the helicopter ascended, the swarm of bats deviated from its flight path, but a few struck the front of the chopper.

"I'm getting her under control," gleaned JP.

"You got this. Great job, my friend," encouraged Felix to JP.

Annie opened her eyes, and she looked below through her window. The helicopter had passed over the density of the forest and was now hovering over a sprawling valley. She saw rolling green hills. The reds, yellows, and purples of all kinds of flowers. Small, reflective ponds coat the grounds. A hawk flew by from the east, soaring high above them.

Something then caught her eye. A shiny glimmer from the edge of the valley. Annie tried to look closer. Then a distinct color stood out.

"I see something," said Annie ominously. "And I think I know what it is."

She pointed out her window. Mrs. Keller, mesmerized by the black swarm of bats circling by the chopper, strained her eyes to see what her daughter saw.

"It looks shiny," said Mrs. Keller.

"And pink," added Annie.

JP tried to hover closer, but the swarm of bats and strong wind made it impossible. He was forced to pull away farther from the valley.

"I'm sorry, gals, I ain't doubling down; we need to head back. We're about ten minutes out from the airfield."

Departing the valley did not matter to Annie. What she saw was unmistakable. A ripped, pink collar with a shiny dog tag. Summer's collar. It stood out like a sore thumb on the green and tan grass. And it meant one thing to Annie: Robin and Summer made it this far. And they were close.

Her gaze at the collar below was interrupted by the blaring of an alarm inside the cockpit. JP and Felix exchanged worried glances.

"I think those bats may have messed up the propellers," said Felix. "This isn't good."

With the high winds surging across the sky, once again, the damaged helicopter struggled to maintain a steady position. Mrs. Keller felt nauseous. She said, "I can't do this a second time."

Annie was beginning to worry the helicopter might not make it to the airfield, but she buried her concerns. It was her turn to be the comforter. "Mom, we are going to be fine."

A new sound accompanied the alarm. A motorized crunching noise. JP looked back at the Keller ladies.

"Hang on!"

The chopper dropped. And dropped. Annie screamed and held her mother's hand for dear life. Mrs. Keller tried to focus on her daughter, but the sudden weightlessness took hold of her whole body. All she could do was grip Annie's hand and pray they would leave this helicopter alive.

"JP, try the throttle!" demanded Felix.

JP nudged it forward. Nothing. The helicopter's propellers were slowing down to a speed that couldn't sustain flying. They were basically in a controlled, bumpy free fall. He continued to work the throttle, hoping the propellers would kick back to life.

"Oh no," said JP.

The wind had escalated. Maintaining an idle position was impossible. JP knew they were doomed if the propellers gave out completely. They needed to make an emergency landing, but they were way past the valley. He tried to spot a clearing, but everything appeared blurry.

Another sudden drop in altitude. Screams echoed throughout the cabin and cockpit. Felix clutched onto his cross necklace, an old Christmas gift from Verona.

"We need to land this thing!" shouted JP.

Annie pointed out her window. "Over there."

Below them, to the east, was a dirty construction site. The ground was coarse in brown and orange mud, with tractors parked throughout the site. JP felt it was a development property for new condos in the backwoods of the Carolinas. But for now, it would have to be their landing zone.

"Here we go, hold on as tight as you can," demanded JP.

They all braced themselves as JP steered the decelerating helicopter to the construction site, hoping to accomplish one of the harrowing landings he's ever had to make. It started to spin in a three-hundred-sixty-degree motion. Smoke billowed from its tail end. The alarms were blaring.

JP demanded again, "Hold on, hold on, hold on!"

Annie screamed. Mrs. Keller screamed. Felix screamed.

The helicopter tail nearly hit a tree just before it touched down mere yards away from a bulldozer, digging deep into the thick mud. One of the propellers nicked a tractor, sending bright sparks into Annie's window.

Everyone in the helicopter cabin was jolted against their seatbelts. Mrs. Keller accidentally bit her lip from the force of the landing. Annie's shoulder felt sore from the belt's resistance.

"Is everyone okay?" asked Felix.

The women were too startled to answer.

JP looked as white as a ghost. He put his hands over his face and said nothing.

"There's not much cell service, but I'm going to try to call Verona," said Felix, still shaken from the landing. "I'll see if she can pick us up in my truck out here. Wherever here is."

JP got his nerves in order. He jumped out of the captain's seat and landed both feet on the ground. He took in a deep breath of air before opening the door for Annie and Francine.

He joked, "Thank you for flying with us; we hope you enjoyed your flight and will fly with us again."

As Annie stepped out, her shoes sunk into the deep mud. She loved it, though. She loved being on safe ground way more than ever before. It was now time to retrieve Summer's collar.

Chapter 27
Too Close for Comfort

Robin and Summer crawled away from their hiding rock. They delved deeper into the shadowy abyss, bumping into unseen scraggly rocks. They had no destination in mind; it was their first time ever exploring a cave.

And it was cold. Really cold. Robin and Summer felt like someone had flipped the seasonal switch, and they were now in the throes of winter. The air felt still yet wet as if it were saturated by hundreds of sprinklers. It all made the dogs shiver.

The worst part was the darkness. It got worse as they furthered away from the entrance. It was the next step above pitch black. Robin looked to his left to stare at Summer; she was only a few feet away, yet he could not see her. As for Summer, she was utterly blinded by the darkness. She tried to follow her brother's lead by sound, but everything had a resounding, confusing echo. It felt like she was trapped in a timeless void.

They weren't the only brave ones to venture this deep into the cave. Summer and Robin could hear and smell the fox getting closer. The fox had better night vision than the dogs.

Summer and Robin attempted to run as the fox gained on them. They could hear its distinct snarling sound. The fox was undoubtedly pestered by the difficulty of catching the dogs. This was no longer a hunt for food; it was a hunt for revenge.

Then, Robin yelped!

The fox had pounced on him. Robin scrambled, screaming and whining as the fox snapped its jaws for the skin. But then there was another pounce.

Summer rammed all her body weight into the two's wrestling match, breaking the fox from his attack. He tried to snap at Summer, missing her body but biting her tail. She yelped in pain. Before he could take another bite, their tumbling turned into a falling.

They had all fallen off a ledge into a deep, dark pool of water. Ice cold water. The dogs struggled to lift their heads above the surface, flailing for air while trying not to drown. Somewhere mixed with them was the fox, also attempting to remain afloat.

The splashing and wails from the animals echoed throughout the cave. Finding the ledge they fell from was like being blindfolded in a water maze. It felt almost impossible.

Robin and Summer were growing weak. The strain in Summer's hind leg made it painful to swim, and her bitten tail made things even worse. The cold water on Robin's snake bite felt like a sharp sting. A scary thought crept into both their minds; this is where they would die.

~

Joey wished he had a louder cowbell. Or maybe a megaphone. The winds coated the sounds of the chimes and whistles. It was a battle against Mother Nature that he knew he would not win.

Mr. Keller felt agony in the pit of his stomach. He was worried about Francine and Annie in the helicopter with how the winds had picked up in the last hour. They had spotted them heading south but never caught them coming back north.

"They probably took a different route," suggested Joey.

Still, the uneasiness remained with Mr. Keller. They should be back by now. His cell phone should be ringing, with his wife telling him they had landed and were okay. Part of him wanted to head back into camp, jump in the minivan, and start searching for them.

Joey could tell his dad was worried. "We can go back, if you'd like, to check on them."

Mr. Keller felt torn. "If we give up the search now, the weather will only worsen as the day goes on. The storm is heading north. This might be our only chance to look around."

The conversation dropped as they heard Joey's name being called. It was coming from the direction of Wilderness World. It was Martha

"Joey! Mitch!" she yelled as she ran through the brush and up to the search party. She was wheezing from how fast she was running.

"Take a breath," advised Mr. Keller. "What's going on?"

"Annie and Francine are back," said Martha. "The pickup truck just rolled up into the driveway. They don't look so good."

They raced back to camp.

Mr. Keller was pleased to see his wife and daughter sitting in the bed of Felix's truck, huddled in a big blanket. Boomer was cuddled next to Annie, snoring. However, as they got closer, he could tell they looked shaken and hurt.

"What happened up there?" asked Mr. Keller. "And what happened to your lip?"

Mrs. Keller responded, "We hit turbulence. We had to make an emergency landing at a construction zone. It was horrible."

"What kind of turbulence?"

"Bats!" yelled Annie. "Thousands of bats."

"The weather report was less than accurate," said Felix. "The storm rolled in quicker then we anticipated. And I'm not sure what drove that swarm of bats to fly out in the daylight, but it was scary. Nevertheless, JP did one job landing us in one piece."

"I never liked the idea from the start. Thank heavens you're all okay," sighed Mitch.

"Well, two good things did come from the trip being a nightmare," replied Fran. "For starters, JP didn't charge us a dime. And because we had to fly so low to the ground, Annie saw something worth interest. "

Annie popped in with glee, "The helicopter ride was worth it because I saw Summer's collar."

Joey was overjoyed. "Where did you see it?"

Annie answered, "I saw it in a valley not far from the mountain and Wilderness World."

Felix added, "But there was no sign of Summer."

Joey's face appeared shocked, as did Mr. Keller's. First Robin's collar by the river, and now Summer's miles onward in the valley.

"Did you see this, Francine?" asked Mr. Keller.

She grimly nodded. "It was her collar, no doubt about it."

Mitchell exhaled. Then he said in a low voice, "My goodness, you were so low to the ground. I hate even imagining it."

"All that matters is we landed and are on the ground now," assured Francine to her worried husband.

Annie added, "We don't have much time left to search on the ground before the storm gets intense. I think it's best we look on the outskirts of the valley for any sign of them."

Edwin chimed in. "There is a hiking trail you can take that will bring you close to that valley. It's a bit of a trek, though, and to Annie's point, Mother Nature and Father Time are not our friends right now."

"We have to try," added Annie.

"I agree," said Joey.

Mr. and Mrs. Keller shared a glance. They both wondered how much longer they could keep up this search. If the collar hadn't been spotted, Mrs. Keller would have suggested that it was game over, that the dogs were gone forever. But the collar renewed a sense of hope in her. To stop trying now would be a regrettable mistake, especially after enduring the helicopter ride from Hell.

"We should give it a look, Mitch," said Mrs. Keller. "Want to continue on with us, Felix?"

"Of course. We can take my truck before hiking it."

Felix loaded his truck up with the Keller family and Martha, who decided to join if the campers weren't going to be allowed. Edwin handed Mitch a physical map of the woods as they loaded up, pinpointing the best spot to reach the valley.

They drove off as the first dark cloud hovered above the camp, killing off some afternoon sunlight. Annie was exhausted, but she knew the dogs were begging to be found.

Chapter 28
Escape

Through the splashes and squealing echoing in the cave, they could hear the familiar hooting of their trusted guardian. The great owl soared through the shadowy walls of the cave, landing on the ledge leading to the dark pool. Still, the dogs could not see him through the blackness.

Hoot, hoot, hoot. To Summer, the owl calls sounded as if they were coming from behind her. She spun her body in a one-hundred-eighty-degree turn, paddling and following for the hoots. Robin followed behind her. And he suspected the fox would follow as well.

Adrenaline and terror had struck their bones. The fox would catch them if they left the pool. It was either die by water or die by the fox. Neither sounded painless. But with two of them, they at least had a chance against the fox.

They were slowly draining energy and stamina, and soon the dark waters would overtake them. They had to move fast. The instinct of survival kicked into gear.

Summer struggled, but she reached the ledge. She could smell the owl; he was hovering above them, merely a step away. She followed him using her sense of smell, and so did Robin. Jagged step by jagged step, they made the climb.

Scratching. Sharp nails against stone and rock. That's what the dogs heard behind them as they ascended the ledge. Using his hind legs, Robin kicked a flurry of pebbles from the ledge, sending mists of sandy cave dirt into the fox's eyes. It stunned him, yelping in pain.

Ungracefully exhausted, the dogs reached over and onto the cave's floor. They had a tiny window of opportunity to escape their hunter, who was blinded and distracted yet again. But this time, there was no cave to hide in. They would be out in the open.

The owl flew through the cave's tunnel. The dogs followed closely, avoiding hitting any of the hidden rocks. Summer briefly tripped from her bad hind leg, but Robin nudged her up to keep going. He would never abandon her again.

A low, groaning snarl came from the back of the cave. The fox had reached the ground floor. The sounds coming from him sounded guttural and vicious. He wanted to *kill* the dogs, his *prey*.

Robin, Summer, and the owl reached outside the cave as their predator rose from the depths and prepared to finish his hunt.

~

"Here it is."

Annie led the walk to the site of Summer's collar. They were all on foot except Felix, who remained at the trail's end with his truck. The Kellers and Martha had to travel off the beaten path to reach the valley. It was an exhausting walk, filled with stumpy groves and thick vines.

But they found it, Summer's collar. The bright pink

fabric was visible in the distance against the greenery. Annie went over to pick it up.

"It's ripped," cried Annie.

The rip was similar to how Robin's collar was torn back at the river. But what ripped Summer's collar?

They all heard a rumbling of thunder. It had been overcast with dark clouds and strong winds since they left camp. To that point, luck had been on their side. Until now.

"We probably have a few minutes before it rains like a monsoon down here," said Martha. "Let's be quick."

They all began combing through the area for signs of Robin and Summer. Checking under logs, through bushes, and behind trees. It did not take long for them to conclude the dogs had moved on.

Annie circled to a ditch in the ground, not too far from Summer's collar. She peered over the edge. "They could be in here."

As she looked inside, she gasped and fell down onto her back. Screaming.

The snake slithered toward Annie menacingly, hissing with a threatening pose. Its forked tongue flickered from its mouth, readying itself to strike.

Both Keller parents were stunned with shock. They were too far from her. They both yelled. "Annie!"

She screamed as the snake bolted to strike. But it never reached Annie.

Joey swung his wrist cast with all his might at the snake's head, sending its whole body flying into the air. It landed somewhere in the shrubbery of the forest.

He helped his sister to her feet. "Close call."

Annie looked at Joey with astonishment. "That was really brave, Joey."

Mr. Keller ran over, with Mrs. Keller and Martha following behind. They checked Annie's legs, arms, neck, and so on for bite marks. She insisted she was okay.

"Joey saved me."

"I guess I did," quipped Joey.

"You kids are going to give me a heart attack," said Mr. Keller.

The moment was interrupted by the incoming droplets of rain. More thunder sounded in the distance, and winds were growing ferociously. They were going to have to leave.

"We should make our way back to the truck," said Martha. "This rain will only draw out more snakes."

As they retreated their steps, Annie held Summer's collar tight in her hand. It had been a crazy, one-of-a-kind day, yet she still came short. No Summer, no Robin. She shivered at the thought the dogs could have possibly ended up in the snake pit.

She turned to Joey. "I want to let you know that if the situation was reversed, I would have hit that snake too."

Joey smiled. "I know you would."

Mrs. Keller said, "I bet Summer and Robin are also defending each other while lost in these woods."

The idea that Summer and Robin were working as a team to get themselves through the dangerous situation of being lost was comforting at first. But then the reality of it all kicked in, for Joey anyway.

"The circumstance is two little dogs are going up against snakes and wild animals, and odds are they don't stand a chance," said Joey with sadness.

Annie took a more positive position. "Anything can happen, Joey. Mom and I were falling from the sky two hours ago with nothing more than luck and prayers on our side. Had you seen it for yourself, you'd bet all your comic books that we'd never be here with you walking the woods. So don't lose faith."

Chapter 29
Face-Off

The forest was engulfed in a gray tone of horror as the storm took hold of the skies. Strong winds surfed through the woods. Rain began coming down in a drizzle, then into a downpour. It was the worst kind of rain the dogs had to face yet.

Injured, thirsty, and hungry, they found it challenging to keep going. But they had to escape the forest once and for all. They knew they were running out of time.

Robin and Summer ran as fast as they could from the cave's opening, scrambling to find a sense of direction in the rainy outdoors. But, before they could determine where to go, both dogs turned back towards the mountain.

The fox had made its way out of the cave. He had bloody cuts and scratches on his body from the bats, and his eyes looked bloodshot. His entire form appeared monstrous. Saliva drooled from his mouth and snout.

For a moment, the dogs and the fox stared each other down. The fox's stare was menacing and villainous. He finally had them in the open, with no means to hide and no means to escape. A devious smirk crept across the fox's face as he lurked toward Robin and Summer.

Hooooooooot...

The owl swooped out of nowhere into the gray sky behind the dogs, striking down with force at the fox. He clawed for the predator's eyes, with his talons cutting the fox's ears and snout. A vicious, protective demeanor overcame the owl. He would not let the fox get to them, not after how far Robin and Summer had made it in the unforgiving forest.

But the fox fought back, snapping at the owl's wings and feet. He bit a chunk of the owl's ear off. The fox would not let the winged cretin disturb his hunt any further.

The dogs were reluctant to leave their guardian behind, but they had no choice. The owl provided them extra time. They had to keep moving.

As they scurried away with their own injuries, the dogs could hear the violent sounds of the owl fighting the fox. The rainfall provided some cover from the noise, but it made it difficult to see far ahead. They trekked in circles and passed patterns of trees, reaching a region of high grass. They crouched in the tall grass, attempting to blend and hide. Summer's leg was swollen to the point there was no seeing the contour of her knee, and her tail was bleeding from the fox's bite. Robin's snake bite was fully infected, with foul-smelling pus beginning to leak from his shoulder.

A shrieking noise erupted through the forest. It sounded like the owl.

Slowly, they peered above the grass. Instantly, they spotted the fox. There was blood around his mouth. The dogs assumed the worst, believing their forest guardian sacrificed himself for their own survival.

The fox was about twenty feet away. He looked deranged, feral, and confused. His nose sniffed aggressively for the whereabouts of his prey, but he failed to pick up any scent; the rain made it too cumbersome. He continued to patrol the forest until he was out of range.

The dogs slinked back into the grass, attempting to decide what to do next. No doubt the fox would be in their position soon to search the high grass. Robin was readying to peek his head out again to see if they could make a break for it when they heard a deep, rumbling noise.

An engine noise specifically. Not a helicopter, but a car engine. And not too distant, either. It sounded like it was getting closer, in fact.

Robin peeked through the grass to spot the noise, but he made a grave mistake.

The fox stood there at face level, mere feet away. Its devilish yellow eyes beamed with anger and hunger. Blood and rain droplets caked his face.

Robin barked.

The fox retaliated by snapping at Robin's face. But Robin retracted quickly, and he and Summer were racing off through the high grass, hoping to lose him. The fox tried to keep up, but his more oversized frame against the thick grass slowed him down.

It occurred to Summer that she should run parallel to Robin, leaving ten feet between them. This would force the fox to pick one trail over the other.

Summer made her move by veering right.

Her path change forced the fox to stop short, as Summer suspected it would. The fox had to choose between dogs; which of his two prey did he want more?

Summer and Robin squandered into further thickets

of high grass. The gap between them and their hunter grew significantly while the fox stood still, making his decision.

Finally, he chose Robin.

Thump. Summer's snout bumped into something crunchy. She looked up; it was a corn stalk. A dozen other stalks were plotted next to the one she collided with. Summer regained her composure and decided she should abandon her plan. She veered left towards Robin, who was quickly limping along a path of corn.

Summer trailed a few feet behind her brother, limping through the corn crop. They had no sense of the fox's whereabouts, but they knew he was close. He would find them easily, Summer feared. The muddy ground was leaving a path of paw prints through the maze of corn.

When the corn ended, Summer and Robin found themselves in a garden filled with plump tomatoes and eggplants. It was all very colorful. The bright reds and purples meshed perfectly.

The dogs limped until they reached another patch. This one offered rows of string beans and zucchini. Robin was so hungry he wanted to stop and bite into something. But Summer knew there was no time to lose. She could faintly hear the fox plowing into the corn stalks. She nudged her brother's rear end with her nose, urging him to pick up the pace.

Circling the garden were fruit bushels of raspberries, blueberries, and blackberries. Robin was leading his sister through it all when suddenly, his eyes caught sight of a prominent structure about a hundred feet away. A large cabin house was within reach, similar to what they saw when they met Whisper and Milton. Only this house was more extensive and different.

Backpacks and toys were lying around the front porch. There was also a breakfast setting arranged at a picnic table under a large overhang next to a dirt parking lot filled with a handful of cars.

It was the first time in days that the dogs had seen a car. A particular vehicle parked in the lot immediately stood out to them. Robin's tail wagged with excitement. Summer's tail wouldn't wag; it was throbbing from the fox bite. But she was just as jubilant as her brother. The vehicle was unmistakable in its shape. It was a minivan.

The rain intensified. The sound of rain droplets belting down on the vegetables made it impossible for Summer to hear the fox rummaging through the corn stalks.

Robin was oblivious to the fox too. Instead, he was enthralled by the rumbling sounds of a truck engine. Summer heard it too. The sound was drawing closer to them, overpowering the thunderous rain. Then the truck drove up in front of the house. The sight of it encouraged Robin to bark. He didn't think of the fox or how the bark would alert him. Summer didn't get mad. How could she? She knew Robin couldn't contain himself; he was too excited.

The fox heard Robin's bark. He was on the right path, and he was very close. Adrenaline kicked in, and the fox went into a runaway sprint.

Summer and Robin could see a group of humans exit the truck; they were wearing raincoats. The humans waved farewell to the driver as they walked towards a larger group of people crowded around a window inside the house.

Under the front porch awning, sheltered from the rain, the two shorter humans looked towards the woods and hollered one last time.

"Robin! Summer! Where are you?"

Robin and Summer's eyes widened with undefinable joy as the humans removed their raincoat hoods.

First Annie. Then Joey. Then Mrs. and Mr. Keller. And then a woman they did not recognize, but it did not matter. The Keller family was within reach, calling their names.

"Robin, Summer, where are you?"

But before the dogs could process the miracle unfolding, they heard another noise. A snarl.

The fox stood menacingly behind them, only a couple feet away. A deep, scabby scratch lined his face from the owl attack. Blood stains remained on the hair on his face. He looked more than predatory; he looked demonic. The fox had grown too tired of this pursuit; he wanted his prey, and he wanted it now. This hunt went on for far too long.

The dogs, re-energized by the sight of their family, jetted through the garden maze, knocking into various berry bushes. The fox loomed behind them, closing in and snapping his jaws at their feet, catching morsels of berries instead of the dogs. The fox then leapt and barreled into them, and they all went tumbling through the last bush.

Summer managed to free herself, but the fox had a hold on Robin. The fox towered over the young cavalier as he lay on his back, preparing to consume his prey. Robin closed his eyes, accepting his fate and hoping his sister would make it to the Kellers.

Instead of escaping to the awning, Summer turned to the fox and aggressively barreled right into him – head first.

The blow from Summer sent the fox flying backward into the garden bushes again. But the fox was too strong and sprung back on his feet immediately. The fox growled at the dogs and dashed for them with ferocious anger.

The fox landed on Robin a second time, the impact more crushing than the first. Robin tried to squirm, but the fox clawed and scratched his stomach. The poor dog yelped with agonizing pain. Summer bit into the fox's neck and hung on for dear life. The fox shifted his weight to throw off Summer, giving Robin a chance to spring to his feet.

Summer was locked into the fox's neck. Robin clawed at the fox's rear end to injure his hind legs. But another rush of adrenaline provided the fox with unbridled fury and strength. He kicked Robin backward and shuck off Summer's bite, flinging the small dog to the ground.

All three animals were tired and wounded, but the fight was far from over. They all re-engaged for another round. They viciously scratched and bit as the rain poured down on them. A blast of thunder roared, and a flash of lightning lit up the sky.

The commotion of it all alerted Joey; he turned his attention towards the garden. He saw the fight unfolding before his eyes. His jaw dropped.

"Robin! Summer!"

Everyone looked in the direction of the dogs as Joey ran towards the fight. Annie chased after him.

"Joey, no! No!" screamed Mrs. Keller from across the parking lot.

Joey defied his mother's orders. And Annie caught up to her brother.

The fox caught a glimpse of the humans running toward him, but he was determined to defeat his prey. Killing Summer and Robin was the only acceptable ending.

Robin was spent, barely able to lift a paw. He sunk to the ground in defeat. Summer tried to last longer. She was not afraid to go toe-to-toe with the huge fox. But her wounded leg had given out. Summer was now on her back, using the one healthy leg to fend off the fox the best she could. But the fox was too strong and too fast. The evil predator clawed at Summer repeatedly.

Helpless, Robin watched as the fox positioned himself for a killing strike on Summer. He was about to bite into Summer's neck when Joey chanted.

"Get off my dogs!"

The demonic fox slowly turned his head toward Joey, and they locked eyes. The young boy was shaking nervously; he was now the target. The fox gritted his teeth as he jumped to strike the young boy's face.

"Don't even try it!" yelled Annie as she jumped in front of her brother and landed a drop-kick to the fox's head. The fox fell to the ground, stunned, then quickly regained his composure. He sprung at Annie, trying to bite her. But Annie was slick. She stepped to the side, causing the fox to miss and fall. She then yanked the fox by its tail and catapulted him yards away.

The fox was unwilling to quit.

He regained himself yet again, and he walked very, very slowly toward Annie. He took his eyes off her for only a moment to notice Summer and Robin. The two dogs were gravely injured, lying motionless on the muddy lawn. The human girl created a barrier, blocking the dogs from the fox's path.

Everyone from the cabin was running over to the lawn, including the Keller parents and Boomer, who was repeatedly barking. The campers used the cowbell, whistles, and clapping to scare off the fox. But the fox would not be deterred.

So many humans all at once; all the loud yelling would usually do the trick in making a wild animal retreat. But not this fox; his desire to kill could not be contained.

Annie was frozen. She didn't know what to do as the fox inched its way closer. The fox's eyes were filled with hunger and anger, and his teeth were as sharp as knives.

Mr. Keller emerged in front of his children. Out of breath from running, he barely got out the words, "Kids, I got this."

Mr. Keller crouched down into a wrestler's position, his hands out in front of him – ready to grapple. The fox was not intimidated by Mitch's size. He inched toward the man – snarling with hatred.

Mitch's heart was racing, but he knew not to reveal his fear. He knew he had to fight fire with fire, so he inched his way toward the fox. Mitch used a deep, steady voice to repeat his warning over and over again, "You better get out of here, Mr. Fox. You better get out of here. Get out of here now, Mr. Fox."

The fox stopped. Mitch stopped. Three feet separated them. They locked eyes.

The fox dug his hind legs into the wet ground. Then, he arched his back end and lowered his head, never taking his eyes off his new prey: Mitchell Keller.

Mitchell's mouth turned dry; the battle with the fox was imminent.

Thunder cracked. Lighting struck a nearby tree. It was time to kill. The fox whined an evil cry, showing Mitch his teeth. Mitchell yelled at the animal, "Don't you try it."

The fox ignored the warning, and he launched into attack.

Cha-chug, boom!

The unmistakable sound of a shotgun firing echoed throughout the campgrounds. Everyone, including Mitch, Joey, and Annie, turned to see Felix standing in the flatbed of his pickup truck. He had seen the animals fighting when driving towards the camp exit. Felix was soaked. He had his shotgun held high – pointing it in the air. Soft wisps of smoke floated out of the gun's barrel.

"Told you this would come in handy," said Felix, addressing the Kellers.

They all turned back to the fox, but he was gone. The thunderous sound of the shotgun sealed the deal. Already deep into the corn stalks, the red-coated predator was heading back to the woods.

Joey, Annie, and the Keller parents finally turned their attention to Robin and Summer.

So many questions arose. How did the dogs make it this far? How did they find the camp? Where did they sleep? What did they *see*? Sadly, they would never get the answers from Robin and Summer. But, if their appearance was any indication, they definitely had been through a lot.

The dogs were found, and they were alive, but this was no time to celebrate. The Kellers could see the damage; their beloved dogs were barely breathing.

Summer and Robin were motionless, their eyes loopy. The bites and scratches along their bodies went from tail to head.

The rain fell on Annie and Joey as they each took a knee beside the dogs. Feeling the presence of the kids, both Summer and Robin simultaneously attempted to stand up and shower Annie and Joey with love. But both dogs succumbed to dehydration, hunger, exhaustion, and injury. Finally, they both fainted in the arms of the Keller children.

Chapter 30
The Prayer

The rain slowed. It was not a light drizzle. For the first time in a long time, Martha ran as if she were a spunky teenager, not someone who could be a grandmother. She ran to the cabin house to call her sister Louisa, the vet. Joey was holding Robin, crying. His dog was not moving. Summer looked terrible as she lay in Annie's arms. Everyone was soaking wet while Mr. Keller ran to the family minivan.

Martha came out of the house. "I called Louisa. She's ready for us, but fallen trees from the storm are blocking the main road. We'll have to take a shortcut."

"Our dad is grabbing the car now," said Annie.

Martha shook her head. "No good. We have to take the dirt roads and trails."

"How?" asked Joey. "The minivan won't be able to drive on that terrain."

Martha turned to Edwin. "Let me take the ATV. It's a four-seater, and we'll get to my sister's clinic in half the time."

"You're gonna drive?" asked Edwin, puzzled.

Martha folded her arms with sass. "Yes, I'm gonna drive it, and I ain't gonna flip it over either. Where are the keys?"

Edwin headed for the infirmary, where he left the keys. Mr. Keller pulled the minivan up.

"What's going on?" he asked.

"We're taking the ATV to the clinic," answered Annie. "It's a shortcut. It'll be faster than taking the roads there."

"Who's we?"

Annie pointed to herself, Joey and Martha.

"If that's the case, I'm coming with you guys," their dad replied as he exited the minivan.

"I'll take the minivan and meet you guys there. Hopefully, the side roads don't take too long," said Mrs. Keller. "Wrap the dogs in the blankets."

She grabbed two blankets from the hatch of the minivan, and the kids wrapped Robin and Summer up like little babies. Half a minute later, Martha was motoring down the driveway in the ATV. She wore a helmet, and three more were on each seat.

"Let's ride, Kellers."

Mr. Keller hopped in the passenger seat, and Joey and Annie went in the back seats, each holding their dogs. They offered words of affirmation, motivating them to hang in there. Both were hardly responsive.

"We need to get going," said Joey anxiously.

"No worries," cautioned Martha. "This reminds me of my days serving in the military. I was the captain of my own Humvee."

Mr. Keller looked at her nervously. "How fast will we be going?"

Before he could finish his question, Martha hit the gas pedal and sped off into the woods' trails. Mrs. Keller hopped in the minivan and plugged in the directions on her

GPS. The ATV was rocketing down the hillside before Mrs. Keller even pulled out of the driveway.

"Oh my God," Mr. Keller silently whispered to himself.

The ATV lurched and heaved over forest mounds, tearing through unmarked trails. The whole experience was bumpy and disorienting; Joey and Annie did their best to hold the dogs securely.

"I may puke," shouted Mr. Keller.

Martha swung a wide turn right down a crescendo of hilly terrain. With a quick left-and-right look, they crossed over a stretch of paved road, assailing deeper into more woods.

"Almost there," yelled Martha.

Joey looked at Robin. His eyes appeared droopy. Summer's eyes were closed, but she shook in Annie's arms.

Martha yelled again, "Hang on!"

The ATV leaped over a four-foot ditch, skyrocketing mid-air. The kids held the dogs tighter and leaned into each other to help stabilize their position. Martha stayed laser focused. Mr. Keller screamed for dear life.

They landed with a thud, and Martha quickly had to dovetail around a twin set of white birch trees. The ATV then sped along a trail designated for bikers.

They rounded a sharp turn on the trail, bringing the ATV into the opening of a field. It was covered in a sea of flowers dotted with yellows, violets, scarlets, and light blues. At the base of the field was a shopping center. The Kellers and Martha could see the two-story office building, their final destination written on a large sign: *Animal Hospital.*

Martha kicked up a gear in the ATV, splashing up rain puddles and further soaking everyone's clothes. They scorched through the flower field; flurries of petals and pollen whipped their faces.

"I have a feeling this is illegal," quipped Mr. Keller.

"Too late now!" shouted Martha.

The rain ended as the ATV roared to the base of the field and into the parking lot. Dozens of people surrounding the shopping center watched in disbelief as Martha pulled up to the front door, even kicking it open.

"Louisa!"

Mr. Keller and the kids, who carried their bundled dogs with them, entered the animal hospital behind Martha. A few people were sitting in the waiting room with their pets, but all the attention was drawn to the Keller family. Their faces were plastered with dirt, grass, and flowers. A long twiggy leaf comically protruded out of Mr. Keller's helmet.

The receptionist stared at them, bewildered. Martha snapped her fingers, breaking the lady's dumbfounded trance.

"We have two cavaliers here that need treatment pronto!"

The receptionist nodded. "Louisa said you were coming. It's a miracle those dogs are alive!"

"They won't be much longer if you don't hurry!" retorted Martha.

A second later, Louisa ran out of her office and to the lobby. "Follow me, Kellers, quickly," she commanded.

Mr. Keller kneeled to Joey and Annie. "I'm gonna wait for your mother to get here. Follow Louisa; I'll be right there."

Mr. Keller gave Robin and Summer kisses on their forehead and then to Joey and Annie. The Keller kids then followed Louisa into the emergency wing of the animal hospital. A creeping sense of bad memories kicked in for Mr. Keller. It reminded him of Zoey all over again.

Louisa motioned the kids into a patient room. She began examining both dogs. She ran temperature checks and observed their injuries. After five minutes, with a sigh, Louisa removed her glasses and addressed the kids.

"Here comes the hard part," said Louisa. "I'm going to have to ask you two to leave. Summer's hind leg is awful, and if not addressed now, she may never walk on all fours again. She also has a bite on her tail and some deep scratch wounds. Tack on severe dehydration; her heart is beating very slowly. Too slowly."

"As for Robin," continued Louisa. "He has an infection from what looks like a snake bite. Along with his scratches and cuts, he too is dehydrated, and he has an elevated fever, and if not treated now, he'll be in even more trouble before the day is over."

Joey cut right to the matter. "What are the odds for each of them to live?"

"I don't have that answer right now, but I will do everything I can to save their lives," promised Louisa.

Two nurses entered the room, masked with scrubs and carrying trays of medical equipment.

"We need to get IV fluids going immediately," Louisa told the staff. "We will have an update for you kids soon. I need you to go outside with your parents now."

Reluctantly, Joey and Annie said goodbye to their dogs, tears forming in their eyes. It could be the last time they ever see them again. They told Summer and Robin how much they loved them and then were escorted back to the waiting room by one of the nurses.

In the waiting room were Martha, Francine, and Mitchell. The kids updated everyone on the condition of Robin and Summer, and they thanked Martha for her efforts. Martha gave Joey a kiss on the head, and then she gave Annie a big hug before leaving with the ATV to return to camp.

The Kellers huddled together as a family in the waiting room.

"They're going to be okay," affirmed Mrs. Keller.

"If those dogs can survive in those woods and storms for three nights, then they can survive anything," added Mr. Keller. "And did you see how they fought off that fox? It was mighty impressive."

Mrs. Keller said, "My gut tells me Summer and Robin are running around full speed in a week."

Joey and Annie weren't buying it. They feared the worst.

"Mom, face it. Robin is going to die. I said goodbye to him before they kicked us out of the room," Joey said as he began crying uncontrollably.

"You have to stay positive, Joey," Mrs. Keeler said with a quiver. She was now crying too.

Annie's face was pale. Her shoulders sagged. She, too, was saying goodbye when the nurses asked the kids to leave. Sure, the dogs were found. The search was over. But the endless pit in her stomach was growing deeper.

Mitchell grabbed his daughter's hand, triggering her emotions to unleash. She was now crying heavily, just like her brother.

"All we can do is hope, dad."

"No, Annie, hope is never enough. We need to pray. The power of prayer should never be denied, and as a family, we have slacked in keeping with our faith. We need to change that, and now is the time to start," said Mr. Keller.

The Keller family had been in this sort of place before with Zoey. They had all *hoped* Zoey would survive, but it wasn't enough. Perhaps prayer would result in a different outcome this time.

Mr. Keller held Annie's hand tighter. He reached his free hand out to Mrs. Keller. She grabbed it. Then she offered her hand to Joey. He grabbed it, and then he offered his free hand to Annie. All of them now holding hands, the family bowed their heads. Mr. Keller led a short but powerful prayer.

"Dear Heavenly Father, we ask you to bless, protect, and heal our beloved Summer and Robin. Humbly, we ask for your divine grace and glory be showered down onto us all. Help us remain together as a family. Amen."

Chapter 31
Reflection

Summer laid still on the hard, steel table. Her eyes were barely open. She winced in pain as Louisa took a look at her leg and hip. It was the worst-case scenario. Her leg had incurred a torn ligament, bone fracture, and compounded sprain. Her hip appeared to be slightly out of its socket. Louisa could not imagine how the dog was walking just hours earlier, let alone fighting off a vicious predator.

It only got worse.

Summer's tail was scratched and bloodied from the fox bite. Her dehydration was approaching borderline fatal, and the scratches throughout her body were severe – some of them would require stitches. The dog had been through a war, thought Louisa.

Across the way, Summer could see Robin; he lay still, his eyes closed. Louisa's assistant was working on him, cleaning his wounds.

Pain surged through Summer, but not from her injuries. It was a pain of heartbreak. They had made it to the end and reunited with the Kellers; now they were on cold, hard operating tables. Both held on by a thread, hoping they would get the chance to live their lives again.

And what a life they have lived so far.

Summer closed her eyes as she thought about the first day she and Robin were brought home from Arnold's farm. It felt like it was only yesterday.

She recalled how Annie went through instructions like a tour guide on parts of the house as if Summer would understand her words. She was nervous for the first few minutes in the Keller house, away from her parents Queen and Chaser. But then she heard Robin and Joey playing in the next room; she was reminded of her brother's presence. He, too, was on this new journey with her. Her nervousness turned into a warm rush. She was feeling the meaning of family.

On the first night at the Keller house, Annie decorated Summer's doggy bed in the corner of her bedroom as if it were a shrine of worship. The bed had an assortment of pink blankets, the cute pink and purple snake toy that looked more like a caterpillar, and even a scent of pet-friendly lavender from her essential oil diffuser. It was the most comforting and welcoming doggy bed of all time.

She reminisced on the nights she would leave her sanctuary of pillows and blankets to cuddle with Annie. Sometimes Annie would be on the phone, gossiping or chatting with friends. Other times it was with her grandparents or distant cousins. Summer didn't understand many of the words, but she loved to listen to the sound of Annie's voice. Sometimes Annie cupped her hand over the phone and talked to Summer as if she were involved in the conversation, like a friend listening in.

One of Summer's favorite memories was when Mr. and Mrs. Keller brought her and Robin to one of Annie's softball games. It was a rough match; Annie's team lost when she was tagged out in the last inning. Annie fell short, sliding into home plate, and her team lost by a single run. She scraped her knee pretty badly on the play. Annie tried to stay strong, but the devastating loss and aching knee pain caused her to wallow. But then she saw Summer and Robin and was instantly happy. Summer tried to lick the wound on Annie's knee as if it would instantly heal the cut.

Joey arrived towards the end of the game following band practice, and the four of them stayed after to run and chase along the bases. Some of Annie's teammates joined in. They ran for hours, never tiring out. Summer soaked in every moment, lapping up every laugh and ear rub.

Summer also remembered the day Annie was preparing to leave for summer camp. She was crying in her room, fearful that she was a bad daughter for failing the promises she made to her parents. Annie hated crying and preferred to do it alone. But Summer could sense her sadness. She cuddled with Annie, nuzzling into her arms to distract her with love. She wagged her tail nonstop – hitting Annie's torso repeatedly until she smiled, which eventually she did.

They remained cuddled together and watched a movie on Annie's laptop. Annie ate popcorn, and Summer chewed on a doggy bone. It was relaxing. It was *home*.

The movie was about a family dog and its wild adventures. At the end of the film, the dog dies. But before it does, the dog recalls all of its fondest memories. And so this made Summer wonder if she, too, was dying. She thought probably so, considering she, too, was running through her favorite memories.

She would give anything to revisit more of her favorite moments again, but Summer's memory reel stopped. Instead, she opened her eyes and focused on the reality she was stuck in. Looking over at Robin, his eyes closed, she knew her brother would soon be thinking back on his favorite moments too.

Robin continued to sift in and out of a dazed state; he could not open his eyes for longer than a second or two. His fever was soaring, and his infection was getting worse. The assistant was getting nowhere, she called Louisa.

Summer's concern elevated, and her heartbeat raced with panic when Louisa ran over to her brother. Robin's body began to shake. Summer winced with sorrow as Louisa injected Robin with a syringe. Within seconds the shaking stopped, and he was very sleepy. He drifted off into his dreams.

Robin dreamt about when he and Joey shared a tent on the RV trip. Joey had asked his dad if he was allowed to sleep one night under the stars instead of inside the camper. His dad agreed though he did not realize Joey planned to bring Robin.

When the campfire died, and everyone turned off their lights, Robin and Joey opened a ceiling flap in the tent and stared out into the night sky, watching the stars. Joey pointed at the different constellations, reciting their names from a book he had once read. Robin watched in amazement as the dark sky was speckled with little lights.

Joey listed off the stars of Orion's Belt: Rigel, Betelgeuse, Bellatrix, Mintaka, Alnilam, Alnitak, Saiph, and

Meissa. None of these names meant anything to Robin, but he was intrigued and bewildered all the same. He was merely a puppy then, but he felt he was introduced to a whole new big world.

A similar feeling was experienced the first snowfall months later. Joey and Annie let the dogs out into the backyard a few nights before Christmas. The air was frigid, but the neighborhood was bedazzled with red, green, and white lights. The dogs were confused at the time why the Kellers were joining them in the cold weather, standing on the back porch in their robes and puffy jackets.

"Should be any minute now, according to the weather app," Joey had said at the time.

And then it happened! The falling of snow. Robin and Summer were covered in it, head to toe. It felt exhilarating and frosty at the same time.

They ran around in the yard, trying to catch the snowflakes with their tongues. Small clumps of snow were already forming over the grass. Robin and Summer peed in the snow, turning white fluff into yellow, much to the amusement of the Keller children.

Robin's fascination with the snowfall equated to his fascination with the stars. Something about the sky had an impact on his mind. But nothing rivaled his favorite memory with Joey. The day at the beach.

It was weeks ago, a few days before they were supposed to leave for camp. It was the same calendar day that Joey and Annie adopted the dogs a year earlier. They were celebrating the anniversary with an after-dinner stroll at the beach.

The softness of the sand on his paws. The salty splash of the incoming surf. Robin was free to do his favorite thing ever on the empty beach. He was free to run!

And boy, did he run. Robin raced up and down the beach in zig zags once Joey let him off the leash. He never strayed too far, but the freedom was immeasurable to anything he had ever experienced. He chased the seagulls; he chased sand crabs; he chased the surf as it swept back into the ocean. If pets made the ultimate decisions in families, Robin would have wanted the Kellers to live in tents on a beach forever.

He eventually tired out after an hour. Full of sand, he resorted to Joey's lap and anxiously waited for whatever came next. The Keller parents started a bonfire and prepared s'mores. Summer was already on Annie's lap, deep asleep, snoring from the exhaustion of running in the dunes.

Robin was given a marshmallow; it tasted superb. His belly was full, and it was time to totally chill out.

Comfy on Joey's lap, Robin watched the waves roll in and then glide out. He nestled his head into Joey's arms but never broke focus from the sea. The miles of blue water meshed perfectly into a pink and yellow sunset. It was inviting to the eyes. Robin was mesmerized by it all and stared out for as long as he could. He fought off sleeping; this moment was too extraordinary to ignore. But his resilience was no match for early evening fatigue, and much like his sister, Robin fell into a deep sleep.

Robin would do anything to be up and about. He didn't want to be in a doggy hospital. He wanted to get up, find Joey, and return to the beach. Or be in a tent staring at the stars. Or be racing around the backyard, chasing snow. But he couldn't move.

Robin's heartbeat dropped, and he felt a cold wave run through his brain. He wanted to bark in fear but couldn't find a way to do it. Then, suddenly, he felt himself lift above his own body, heading towards a white light. He looked down and saw himself lying on the operating table; Louisa repeatedly yelled his name: *Robin! Robin! Robin!*

He was leaving this earth, he could feel it, but he didn't want to go. Robin resisted the light. He pushed back against the vacuum, sucking him into the bright white sky.

"His heart rate is picking up; we need to stabilize," Louisa called out.

Robin's resistance to the light was working; he was inching his way back. He was heading downward, moving towards himself on the operating table, away from the white light. He could hear Louisa say, "I've got his heart going again, but I don't know how long I can keep it going."

Robin was back inside his body, but the pain was unbearable. Somehow he found the strength to peek his eyes open. He saw his sister at a similar table across from him. Summer's eyes were closed.

Louisa yelled, "Damn it, I am losing him again."

The white light was coming after him again. He strained to keep his eyes open; if this was the end, he needed to see his sister. He would be content if she was the last thing he ever saw. The light was getting brighter, and Louisa yelled louder, but Robin was calm because Summer was in his sight. And then suddenly, Summer opened her eyes and connected with Robin.

They looked into each other's eyes. Robin told Summer through his stare that he wouldn't want any other dog in the world on this journey with him. He told her he loved her and that she was beautiful and thanked her for fighting for him until the bitter end.

Summer responded with a warm stare of her own. She told Robin they were tighter than a perfect-fitting glove. They were like Joey and Annie. Their bond was inseparable, and no matter where they were – even if it was worlds apart – they would always be together in spirit like every brother and sister should be.

Robin formed a tear in his eye. He knew it was time to go.

Louisa called his name again. "Robin! Come on boy, come on Robin, don't leave me, don't you dare leave Joey."

Summer tried to wiggle her tail, and she tried to lift her paw. She needed to get herself up off the table and help her brother. But she couldn't move. She was too weak.

Summer sent her brother a sad-filled look, her eyes welling up with tears knowing this was goodbye. Robin couldn't bear to look her way. It was too heart-wrenching. He closed his eyes slowly. And at that very moment, Summer decided she, too, was ready to leave this earth. The pain throughout her body, the pain in her heart, it was all too much. She loved Annie, Joey, Mitchell, and Fran, but Robin was her blood. They were born together. More importantly, they survived the woods together. And that was something they could have never done alone. Therefore, she needed to be with him wherever he was heading.

Robin closed his eyes. Summer's eyes closed shut too. Louisa continued to call out to Robin. Nothing was working.

Louisa bowed her head. She asked herself, "How am I going to face those children?"

Chapter 32
Fighting the Odds

The Kellers stood up from their chairs as Louisa entered the lobby. Her face portrayed a guarded look. Joey and Annie couldn't tell if they were about to receive good or bad news.

"I know you're all anxious for an update," said Louisa. She flipped open her clipboard.

"Summer has a bite mark on her tail. From what we can see, it's likely from the fox. The tail needed stitches, as did countless cuts throughout her midsection. The cuts are infected, making things even worse. But the real concern is whether she now has rabies. She also has multiple problems with her hind leg and hip. And I'll do everything I can to save the leg, but we won't know the results tonight. Tack on the internal damage from a lack of food and water for so many days, and it's a lot for a young dog – it would be a lot for any dog. I simply do not understand how she made it this far."

Annie asked, "Will she live?"

Louisa replied with little confidence, "On a scale of one to ten, ten being the best, I would put her at a three, maybe a four. We got her to stabilize moments before I came out here, but I will not lie to you. The odds of full recovery are low right now. And if she does survive, her leg may never heal correctly. In fact, she may have to lose her leg."

Annie went to ask another question, but Joey chimed in. "What about Robin?"

Louisa, an unusually tall woman like her sister Martha, took a knee to be at eye level with Joey.

"Robin is the toughest dog I've met, and that means a ton considering we have no shortage of pit bulls in this town. But Joey, much like Summer, Robin came in here with deep cuts and scratches all over his body, including a nasty wound on his snout from what looks like a porcupine quill. But he isn't as hardy as Summer. So, it takes a toll when a dog of his size goes without food and water. And when combined with the venom from the snake bite on his shoulder, his little heart is up against a fight that is nearly impossible to win. With that said, I actually saved him from cardiac arrest twice. But it's not enough. My bet is it will happen again. Plus, his elevated fever won't come down. Ultimately, Joey, odds are it will all be too much for Robin to overcome. So, we don't want to be unfair to him. Do you understand what I am saying?"

Joey's eyes welled up with tears. He asked Louisa, "Are you saying you can't save Robin? Is my dog going to die today?"

The little boy's question and how he asked it sent a chill down Louisa's neck. She was a professional, she didn't get emotional about her patients, but suddenly she found herself fighting off the tears. She took a deep breath. She held it. She didn't want to answer the boy.

Joey grabbed her hand, "Tell me my dog is going to live! Please! I am begging you."

Joey's tears rolled down his cheeks. Louisa looked away from Joey and took another deep breath to gain her composure. She put down her clipboard. She needed the free hand to wipe the tears from Joey's face.

"Robin's heart is barely beating, and I fear it won't last much longer. I have tried everything, Joey, and as much as you love him, we need to recognize that if he wakes up, he will be frail. And likely in a lot of pain."

Joey pulled away from Louisa and ran to his father to be hugged.

Mrs. Keller, crying herself at this point, asked, "What are you suggesting, Louisa?"

"As a family, you should consider putting him down."

Joey broke from his father's hug and screamed, "No!"

The young boy darted towards the operating room, determined to be with his dog. Annie followed in a sprint. She wanted to be with Summer.

Chapter 33
The Lullaby

Francine, Mitchell, and Louisa entered the operating room. Louisa's assistant looked like a deer in headlights. She said, "I am sorry, Louisa, I didn't have the heart to tell the kids they couldn't come in."

Louisa responded, "I totally understand. Let's you and me go out to the hallway and give the family some time alone."

Joey was weeping. He stood over Robin, rubbing his back.

"I love you, Robin. I love you so much. I tried so hard to find you. I am sorry it took so long; I am sorry this is happening. Please do not leave me. Please do not go to Heaven, not yet. We have so much more to do together."

Fran grabbed Mitchell's hand. She needed his strength and support. She was feeling equal parts sorrow and guilt. The guilt stemmed from her role in allowing the dogs to be lost in the first place.

Mitchell leaned in and kissed Francine's forehead, then whispered in her ear, "We did all we could."

Annie stood at Summer's side. There were so many wounds, so many stitches. Annie was too afraid to touch Summer. Her dog looked so fragile.

Joey asked his father to sing the lullaby. It's the one Mitchell would sing to Joey as a little boy when nightmares kept him from sleeping. The song is generational because Mitchell's father sang it to him as a boy.

The lullaby tells the story of an Army soldier shipping off to war, and he instructs his young son to take care of his family while he's gone. When and if the soldier will return to his son is unknown, so there's a sad finality to the lullaby – but the farewell is filled with love.

Mitchell always altered the words, making them unique to the original version. He did this to fit into Joey's situation at the time. And the lullaby always made Joey feel at rest, and he would fall asleep peacefully.

Standing mere feet from his son, daughter, Summer, and Robin, Mitchell sang the lullaby in a soft voice, changing some of the lyrics to fit the situation.

Go to sleep, boy; it's getting late.
My watch says it's half past eight.
In an hour, I must go.
When will we unite? Well, I don't know.

While I'm gone, you'll be the man.
Help your sister when you can.
It's a big job, I can see.
For a dog who's barely three.

Beloved Robin, I give you a kiss.
It's my way to say you I shall miss.
It's okay now; close your eyes.
No need to see me when I cry.

So go to sleep, boy, it's getting late.
Dream of times when times were great.
In an hour, I must go.
But my love for you will always grow.

Annie ran over to Joey and hugged him from behind. Joey's eyes fixed on Robin; he petted his dog with tenderness. Joey sobbed softly, in the way that only happens when a loved one is leaving forever.

Mitchell suggested gently, "I think it is time to say goodbye."

Joey looked at his father.

"Dad, unlike the song, I am not leaving in an hour. I am not going anywhere; I am staying right here, and so is Annie. She will stay with Summer, and I will stay petting Robin until he wakes up."

"Oh, Joey, I know it hurts, but we've got to let go," replied his mother.

"No, mom, I can feel him. Daddy, I can feel his heart telling me Robin still has some fight left. All he needs is more prayers and love, and he needs me to be by his side. He is going to live, and Summer is too. Our dogs are going to live no matter what anyone says differently. I know it, Annie knows it, and you need to believe it."

~

Louisa and the Keller parents spoke in the hallway while Joey and Annie remained in the operating room.

"I'm so sorry, Louisa. I know you have to go home to your family. But I don't know how to pull them away," said Mr. Keller.

"Mitchell, first let me say I ain't leaving these dogs alone. I will sleep here tonight if I must. Second, I've been doing this a long time, and my heart is aching for your children in a way it's never ached," replied Louisa. "If I had to put my finger on it, there is something special and magical about those dogs and their connection with your son and daughter. So, although it's against my house rules, I'm willing to break those rules. I'm fine with allowing the kids to remain in the room by themselves for another hour."

Francine asked, "Do you think Robin can make it another hour?"

"If he does, it will be a miracle."

"What about Summer?" asked Mitch.

"I'm pretty sure she makes it through the night, and if she does, her chances of survival go up exponentially, but it will take a miracle to save that leg," responded Louisa.

Mr. Keller looked through the small glass window on the operating room door. He could see Joey and Annie. Both kids sat on small stools, each placed as close to the tables as possible. The kids expressed love for the dogs and prayed for a miracle.

Chapter 34
Dynamic Duo

After a long dinner at a local diner, the Kellers returned to the camp to thank everyone for helping in the search for Robin and Summer. Plus, they had to get their bags from the guest cabin. On the drive over, Mrs. Keller called Louisa for an update.

Two hours had passed, and both dogs were still alive. Louisa said Summer was stable, but Robin was hanging on by a thread. He showed no sign of improvement. Maybe he would live another hour or two, she guessed.

Joey asked from the backseat, "What did Louisa say?"

Francine told the truth, but with a twist. "Summer is stable, but the next few hours are critical for Robin."

Joey smiled wide. "He made it past the first hour, Louisa was wrong, and I was correct."

Mr. Keller looked through his rearview mirror, concerned; he didn't want Joey's hopes to get high.

"Dad, don't worry. Robin is going to make it. And I told him how to do it."

"How so?" asked Mitch.

"I reminded him of a comic book story where Batman and Robin were facing a fight against the biggest and meanest criminals ever to storm Gotham City. They were outnumbered, and nobody thought they could win. The police chief and the mayor were prepared to hand over the keys to the city. Robin asked Batman what they should do. Batman said the plan was to think positive and not to listen to the naysayers who didn't believe the dynamic duo would prevail," boasted Joey.

"So what happened next?" asked Mitchell.

Joey answered, "A few hours later, Batman and Robin faced off against the villains. They were outnumbered, even more than expected. They took some bruises, but they fought with everything they had. In the end, they won. They never accepted losing as an option."

"What's the point?" asked Annie.

"The point is the same positive thinking is at work here," claimed Joey.

He continued, "When I left Robin, I told him Louisa didn't think he would make it through – that he wouldn't make it another hour. I told him we'd prove her wrong. Just like Batman and Robin overcame the odds, we would too. And therefore, I expected him to live up to his name and fight like a superhero. I reminded him that's why I named him Robin. He's my partner. We're a dynamic duo. And superheroes never give up, they always think positive, they always beat the odds, they always win."

"Is that all you told him?" asked Francine.

Joey responded, "I also told Robin that I loved him, and I promised that if he could make it past the hour, he'd make it all the way. And then I gave him a kiss, just like in dad's lullaby, but I told him I knew when I'd be back."

Francine asked, "And when is that?"

Joey smiled. "Tomorrow morning."

When the Keller minivan pulled up to the cabin, all the campers came running out. As did Martha, Edwin, and Boomer. Felix and Verona were there too.

Mitch provided a detailed synopsis of the situation.

"We are confident in the team at the animal hospital; your sister is a wonderful veterinarian, Martha. But we must wait and see what the next few hours bring for Robin and Summer. In short, it's a waiting game none of us want to play, but we are fortunate to be in it," explained Mitchell.

Everyone nodded as if they fully understood the gravity of the situation.

Mrs. Keller indicated they were all exhausted and couldn't stay. The Keller clan planned to check in at the hotel across the street from Louisa's clinic.

The entire family thanked Martha and Edwin for all they had done.

Martha responded, "You are more than welcome to stay here another night."

Francine answered, "Thank you so much, but the kids want to be super close to the dogs."

"I totally understand," said Martha. "And please, do not worry about updating us. You have your hands full as it is. Louisa will fill me in on the details at some point. Just know we are praying for Summer, Robin, and your entire family."

"Thank you," replied Francine.

The kids also bid farewell to their camp buddies and Boomer, and they all promised to keep in touch. Austin and

Oliver signed Joey's arm cast, prompting more campers to do the same.

Before the Keller family took off, Felix made a generous offer to Mitch.

"Mitch, if the dogs end up staying at the clinic for a long time, you are more than welcome to stay with us free of charge. No need to pay for a hotel."

Mitchell responded, "I can't tell you how much we appreciate the offer, Felix. Everyone is being so kind to us. Even my old employee Harold came out of retirement to cover for me at the store."

Mr. Keller's response was interrupted by his phone ringing. Caller ID showed it was Louisa. A sick feeling took over his insides.

"Is it Louisa?" asked Annie.

"No, Annie, it's Harold," lied Mitchell. "Let me take this in private; he is probably asking about the security alarm code. I changed the numbers after he left for retirement."

Mitchell hated lying to his daughter, but it was a white lie. The kind of lie that helps a person versus hurting them. If life had ended for Summer or Robin, it would be terrible news to deliver in front of everyone.

Walking away from the crowd, Mitchell took the call.

"Hello, this is Mitchell."

"Hi, Mr. Keller. This is Louisa. I'm afraid I have some news to share."

Mr. Keller let out a big sigh. He hadn't prepared himself for the worst.

"I'm all ears, Louisa."

"Mr. Keller, I will start with the good news. Summer does not have rabies. She is going to make it through the night. I am sure of it."

Mitchell responded, "What's the bad news?"

"Summer's leg requires surgery. I will do everything I can to save it, but it may need an amputation. I want to get your consent before starting."

Mitchell followed up with another question. "What is her best-case scenario?"

Martha sighed. "The best case is I save the leg, and she limps for the rest of her life. The biggest downside is a heart attack during the surgery; it's always a risk. But in Summer's case, the risk is a bit higher, considering all she's gone through. I must also tell you this is not cheap to do. Therefore, I will need you to sign a waiver and consent form."

Mitch took a deep breath.

"I understand the downsides. I understand the cost. But Summer is a strong dog. So let's do the surgery," confirmed Mitch.

He followed up with another question, "How about Robin?"

Silence took over.

"Louisa?"

"Yes, Mr. Keller, I am here."

Mitchell spoke softly. "You can tell me."

"I have tried everything to bring down his temperature, but it's not working. Any other dog, the fight would have been long over by now."

Mitchell asked, "What's the timeline?"

"I told you he wouldn't make it an hour. I was wrong. So, I dare not place a bet of time against this dog's will to live. But again, unless there is a miracle, I think you should spend the evening preparing Joey for the worst," explained Louisa.

"We are staying with Felix. Should I stop in on the way to sign the form? I can be there in fifteen minutes," suggested Mitchell.

"Yes, great idea. But please don't bring the kids inside. It would be too much right now."

"Not a problem," declared Mitchell.

~

There was silence for most of the ride to the animal hospital. Joey and Annie were mentally exhausted. Francine had a splitting headache, and Mitchell wanted to avoid conversations about Robin's chances or Summer's surgery.

Mitchell pulled the car into the clinic parking lot. He spewed another white lie, "I think I left my wallet in the waiting room. You all stay here; I will be right back."

"Can we see the dogs?" asked Joey.

"No, pal. We can't."

Mitchell never lied. But in a matter of thirty minutes, he had told two fibs. Francine sensed there was something wrong; there was no way her husband had left his wallet inside the hospital. But she didn't dare ask for details, not with the kids listening to every word from the back seats.

"Do you think they're getting better?" asked Annie.

Mitchell was unwilling to lie a third time.

"I don't know, Annie. We have to pray for the best and prepare for the worst. But we also must recognize that sometimes life isn't fair, no matter how hard we pray."

Mitchell exited the minivan.

While sitting outside the animal hospital, Joey noticed something out his window. It was a great horned owl, also known as the tiger owl. It had a strange-looking ear – *only half an ear* – as if it had been recently bitten. But even so, the owl was perched on a lamppost next to the building, guarding whatever was inside. Joey recalled in one of his books that owls were protectors of the woods and were blessed with wisdom. He took the owl's presence as a sign of good luck.

Mr. Keller signed the release form and asked to see the dogs.

Louisa brought him into a room where Summer and Robin lay with their eyes closed. Mitchell walked over to Summer. He lightly petted the top of her head.

"You're such a good girl, Summer."

She slowly opened her eyelids. Mitchell could tell she recognized him but was too pained to move. She tried to show her love and affection by staring into Mitchell's eyes. But holding her eyelids open for more than a few seconds was a task. She quickly drifted back to a state of rest.

Mitch turned his attention to Robin. The dog was motionless. The only sound from Robin's side of the room was the drip from the IV bag. Mitchell's eyes began to water as he walked over to the young dog.

"Can I touch him?" asked Mitchell.

"Yes, you can," said Louisa.

Mitchell tried to find an area to rub. But Robin's entire body was wounded. His front right shoulder and leg were fully wrapped in gauze bandages. A needle was taped to his right hind leg. Robin looked terrible. The little dog was fading away.

Mitchell lowered himself down to Robin's right ear. He whispered, "I know you can hear me, Robin. We are praying for a miracle, and that miracle is you."

A tear fell from Mitchell's face as he kissed Robin's head.

Epilogue
Winter

The scent of coconut plumed from the bath bubbles. Its aroma filled the small bathroom as the soap formed into mountains of white suds. The warm water carried a heap of it to the edge of the bath.

Annie took a scoop of the soapy foam and splashed it against her face. She looked like Santa Claus. Joey took a scoop, plopped it on his head, and coated more around his chin. He appeared as Albert Einstein or some crazy scientist.

Joey then blew one of the bubbles from his hand, the one that used to have a cast. It floated through the air mystically until Summer jumped up and nipped the bubble, sending splashes of bath water all over Joey and Annie.

"Summer, easy on the leg, crazy girl!" called Annie.

They weren't the only ones voicing disapproval at Summer. Her equally devious brother, Robin, barked at her before climbing to the bath's edge and trying to eat the bubbles off Joey's chin.

"Settle, boy, settle!" said Joey.

Mrs. Keller opened the door to the bathroom. "Is everything okay here?"

"We're fine, mom," answered Annie. "We're almost done giving the dogs their bath."

Mrs. Keller nodded. "Make sure you're careful when you dry off Summer's leg. But hurry up; your father and I are ready to decorate the Christmas tree."

"Just make sure dad doesn't eat the cookies I left out for Santa," joked Joey.

"No promises!" Mr. Keller shouted from the other room.

Mrs. Keller closed the door, leaving the kids to finish their soapy task. Joey and Annie spent the night bathing and washing the dogs.

"I'm never taking my eyes off these two again," said Annie. "If we're going to camp next year, they are coming with us."

"I agree with that," said Joey. He looked at the scar on Robin's shoulder from the snake bite. It was healing quicker than expected.

Joey said, "I can't believe it. I think his shoulder will be normal by Valentine's Day."

Annie smiled. She playfully patted Summer and Robin and then began drying the dogs off from their bath.

"Don't forget to give them the Miracle Me!" Mr. Keller shouted.

Summer's leg was healing as Louisa said it would post-surgery. And the inflammation was going down considerably each week with help from *the bottle of magic*. That's what Louisa called the bottle of Miracle Me CBD Pet tincture. Robin was using it, too, every day.

"Come here, Robin," Annie instructed.

Annie gave Robin a biscuit treat peppered with the liquid from the Miracle Me CBD Pet tincture bottle. He ate it up, loving every bite.

"Every dog in the world should be using this stuff," said Joey.

Robin's survival was a total miracle, claimed Louisa. His fever broke shortly after Mitchell's kiss at the hospital. Louisa said she had never seen anything like it. And Robin's shoulder had significantly recovered by Thanksgiving, and it was getting better each week. So too, were all the cuts and deep scratches on both dogs.

Each day since arriving home, the Keller family had been diligent in taking care of the dogs. They followed Louisa's instructions perfectly. In the mornings, they would rub some of the liquid on the scars and scratches. They'd give it to the dogs orally at night, usually by mixing it in with a treat. And as a result, the healing process was undeniable. All the aches, pains, and swelling were no match for the magic bottle.

"This bottle is truly filled with miracles," said Annie as she gave Summer her nightly dose of Miracle Me CBD Pet tincture.

~

The Kellers had settled in. They were ready to spend the night decorating their tree while eating snacks and listening to Christmas music.

Annie climbed the ladder to the top. She needed the height to place the last ornament on the Christmas tree – the golden Keller star. It was always the final decoration set every year.

Joey sat on the floor, petting and massaging the ears of Robin and Summer. When they weren't yearning for human affection, they were tug-o-warring over a squeaky toy octopus. It was their shared early Christmas gift from Joey and Annie, along with peanut butter-flavored dog treats and new walking leashes. The dogs were also given brand-new collars and engraved dog tags.

Francine asked her husband to photograph the dogs in front of the tree. But before he could respond, Mitch's phone rang.

"It's my brother, Dale," said Mitchell.

"Put him on speaker phone," urged Francine.

"Merry Christmas, Dale," chimed Mitchell. "Everybody is here."

"Merry Christmas, Keller family," shouted Dale. "When are you all coming to visit us?"

"Uncle Dale, can we visit the Grand Canyon?" asked Joey.

"Absolutely, it's only an hour north of me," responded Dale.

"The budget's a bit tight right now, Dale," inserted Mitchell. "But if things pick up at work this winter, maybe we can visit for a week."

"Great news!" exclaimed Dale. "We'll have the rooms set for all four of you."

"Six of us," chimed in Francine. "Our dogs are coming too, no exceptions."

Dale chuckled. "I love it; I've been waiting to meet Summer and Robin."

Annie inserted, "Uncle Dale, you're going to love them."

"I'm sure I will. They can hang out with my dogs," said Dale.

"Perfect," added Mitchell before ending the call. "We'll see you soon. Merry Christmas, brother, give our love to the family!"

It had been a few months since the incident during camp. Annie and Joey were doing great in school – keeping up their grades, playing sports, volunteering, and remaining diligent with completing house duties and chores. Most importantly, they learned to balance these priorities and did a much better job caring for Summer and Robin.

"Excellent job placing the Keller star, Annie," said Mr. Keller from the couch. He took a sip of egg nog. "One day, you and Joey won't need the ladder."

Mitchell stood up and closed the ladder. "I'm going to get this out of the way and bring it back to the shed."

"Hurry back," ushered Francine. "It's cold out there tonight."

Mr. Keller laced up his boots and embarked on the snowy Christmas Eve night to return the ladder. The snowstorm started hours ago, ideally in time for Christmas morning.

Robin and Summer started tussling and chewing at the toy octopus. Then they got distracted and tried nibbling at their own doggy Christmas sweaters. Robin's was red and green, and knitted across the torso was the expression, *San-*

ta's on the Woof! Summer's was pink and white, with the knitted caption, *Don't pee on the Christmas tree!*

The dogs got caught up in the bliss of their nibbling. They turned and laid on their backs to welcome any and all belly rubs. Both Joey and Annie volunteered.

Mrs. Keller smiled. "It's crazy to think that I almost lost them."

Annie smiled back at her mother. "You didn't, though, mom. Our prayers were answered, and that's all that matters now."

Joey nodded in agreement.

Both Joey and Annie stood up and hugged their mom tightly. The dogs noticed the action and wanted in on the spread of affection. They all laughed as Robin and Summer tried to wiggle their way into the group hug when Mr. Keller opened the door.

Something was snuggled into his arms. His face displayed worry. And the dogs picked up a new scent.

"You're not going to believe this," declared Mitchell.

Francine looked at him quizzically. "What's that in your scarf?"

His scarf was tucked into a shelter of incubation within his arms. Something moved underneath it, and then its head popped up.

A kitten. Striped with gray and white patterns, with big blue eyes. She looked afraid and lonely. She had frozen snow on her paws.

"This little kitten was out by the shed," said Mr.

Keller. "No mama cat or anything. No collar or name tag. She looked cold, so I just thought to bring her in."

Both Joey and Annie smiled.

Francine said, "It's the dead of winter out there. Let's get her warm!"

They wrapped the little kitten in a small afghan blanket, cozying her by the fire. Francine poured milk into a bowl for the little kitty, which she lapped up lavishly.

"What should we name her?" asked Joey.

Annie looked at the kitten's beautiful blue eyes. "Winter."

Robin and Summer cautiously strolled up to sniff and examine the new feline in their house. The small cat reminded them of their much larger friend, Whisper. They both tuned in closer to the kitten with their snouts; it playfully licked their noses, and the dogs licked back.

The kitten then slumbered into a nap. Robin and Summer eyed the new family member with curiosity but mainly with a sense of protectiveness and affection. They wondered about all the future mischiefs and adventures they would get into with their new sister, Winter the miracle cat.

"Looks like we'll have seven of us visiting Uncle Dale next summer," joked Joey.

The four Kellers, their two dogs, and their newly adopted kitten snuggled together on the family couch, enjoying the sweet scents and sounds of a Christmas Eve night.

Acknowledgments

The creation of this work of fiction would not have been possible without the genuine efforts of my loving family. To my siblings, Ashley, Ryan, and Kelly, thank you for always having my back and providing input on new ideas. I might be the oldest, but I learn from you guys every day.

And the greatest thank you is owed to my parents. Both my mom and dad stand to be why I am the person I am today. Without their unconditional support and love, this novel would not exist. For that, I am forever grateful to be your son.

The funding for this work was made possible by TeamDML Inc., and Miracle Me USA, LLC. The CBD product, Miracle Me CBD Pet tincture, described in the book is genuine. Learn more about the company's unique products for people and pets by visiting MiracleMeUSA.com.

Finally, a much-needed declaration of appreciation to the two stars of the show – Robin and Summer! While their actions in the forest are fictitious, many situations that unfold before they become lost and after they are found are inspired by actual events. Robin and Summer are brother and sister, and their adorable and lovable personalities are very much real. There were plenty of times in the writing of this book when one of those two dogs would lay on my lap as I would type away. Besides being the ultimate source of inspiration, Robin and Summer are the best pets any family could ask for. I'm glad my family is stuck with them.

About the Author

Denny Lynch originally grew up on the shores of Long Island, N.Y., before trading the northeast for sunny West Palm Beach, Florida. At 27, Lynch has assisted in the works of numerous books and documentaries, *The Wild Adventures of Robin and Summer* is his first published novel.

On weekends, Lynch likes boating, swimming at the beach, or practicing golf. He's seen much of the United States but hopes to explore and visit new places to inspire more ideas for his next book.

And, of course, one of his favorite pastimes is to take his dog, Robin, for long walks around his neighborhood, and Summer, too, whenever Lynch visits his family. As of August 2022, Robin and Summer are three years old and healthy as ever. To learn more about them by viewing photos and videos, and to track future projects, please go to DMLbooks.com